STANDING
IN THE
SHADOW

CHARLIE BARNETT

Book Cover Design by Melvin Barnett

ISBN-978-0615557939

Printed in the United States of America

Contents

Prologue

The year is 1873. Let me introduce you to a well established family in Carterville, Illinois, doing what has to be done and growing older, with very little excitement in their lives. William Blunt owns the hardware store in town and his wife, Elizabeth, works with him part time, keeping the books. They have a fourteen year old son - a well groomed, young man who is in church every Sunday.

Mr. Blunts hobbies are repairing guns and reloading his own caissons. Elizabeth enjoys tending her flowers and church work. Now, Billy, the son, loves to read "Wild West" books that feature Wyatt Earp and Doc Holiday. His mother hates his reading interests; she wants Billy to be a preacher or a doctor. She also hates guns - pistols and rifles alike; if it makes a noise she hates it.

Sad to say, every chance Billy gets he is practicing his fast draw with a Colt peacemaker from his father's gun shop. Billy is dare some to let his mother see him with a pistol... he even hides his "Wild West" novels from her.

After Elizabeth's mother and father pass on, she goes into a state of depression. When her husband and son want to move west, she agrees a change of scenery might help. Fort Worth, Texas will be their new home.

Billy stands in his father's shadow until the bitter end. His many opportunities to advance his skill in becoming a lawman, even a U.S. Marshal, soon diminish.

Chapter One

Moving To Fort Worth

If you had lived in or around the Fort Worth, Texas area during the year 1873, you would have experienced law and order, and most likely you would have met and known a great man...William Blunt, U. S. Marshal.. He was a happily married man, and also my father.

Hello, I am Billy Blunt, a chip off the old block. My mother hates that cliché with a purple passion, but that is the scuttlebutt around Fort Worth nowadays, at least among the old-timers the age of my father.

The story you are about to read didn't start in Fort Worth but in Carterville, Illinois. This is where I was born and raised, until I was fifteen-years old. My father owned a successful hardware store and gun repair shop on the side. One thing I remember from my childhood was my father's infatuation with guns. Rifles or pistols - he had this passion for guns...one could say it grew into his hobby.

On the other hand, my mother, Elizabeth, hated guns. Rifles or pistols - if they made a noise she hated them. I actually believe my mother would have washed my mouth out with a bar of lye soap if I had even mentioned guns in her presence, let alone in our house.

Now don't get me wrong or jump to any off the wall conclusion; my mother was a good wife to Father, and a good mother to me. She was very loving, and the best cook in the state...She just didn't have any use for guns...I hope I've made my point. My father was a gunsmith when she married him. This alone boggles my mind... I guess she thought in some way her love could change his love for guns. Well...it didn't and there was always that wedge between them - firearms.

I never could see what all the commotion an' complaining was about; Father made a fine living at the hardware and gun shop. Why we had the most expensive house in Carterville, Illinois. My mother and father were in church every Sunday morning that rolled around -. Whether it be rain or shine. Mother said we were good Methodists and the preacher was always welcome at out home; Pastor John Boggs did come by every chance he could get away from his pastoral duties.

Mother had been taught this Bible verse - 'if you live by the sword, you will die by the sword'...course Mother turned it around to fit her fancy...if you live by the gun, you will die by the gun. My father was as good with a gun as anyone, and he knew all about gun repair. He had the tools to build broken parts for guns, and he reloaded his own cartridges.

A few months after Grandfather and Grandmother Morley (my mother's parents) passed on; it appeared that Mother went into a state of depression. Father got the notion to go out west, thinking the change of scenery might help Mother. I think this was a long time dream of his - to open a hardware store and gun shop - someplace in the "Wild, Wild West".

My mother was the sentimental type and loved her mother and father dearly. I remember being amazed that Grandmother and Grandfather died within a month of each other. Mother, being so close to them, an' all, took their deaths very hard. I guess she also thought getting out of Carterville, Illinois and changing to western scenery would be the wisest path for her at this time.

Nevertheless, Mother agreed to Father's whims, wants and wishes, and began packing to go west. I was young, and didn't understand the complications of a transaction of this magnitude. Naturally, Father had to sell his hardware store and the house we were living in. If I remember correctly, Mother was more interested in what the town of Fort Worth, where the family would call home, would be like. Would they find a church? What about a proper school? Would she make friends with the ladies of the local flower club and enjoy tea time with them?

Father didn't go into this venture blindfolded. He had done his homework by sending a few telegrams...seems his choice of a place to settle was Fort Worth, Texas. According to him it was a growing town. This he explained to mother at breakfast. The town at the time didn't have a hardware store or gun shop...the down side - by the time we moved there and settled down, it didn't have a sheriff either. We found out the sheriff had been gunned down on Main Street by a rowdy cowboy on a trail drive. This seemed not to upset mother at the time; she had her mind on a beautiful house and flower garden.

I'll admit Father knew guns, but he knew nothing about being a sheriff. It was at least two months that men worked every day building father's hardware store, and it took nearly that long to get it stocked the way Father wanted it. You could say things sped up after the railroad came through Fort Worth.

Of course, Mother got her foot in the door at the school and she started a flower club from scratch. Mother and Father both made it their first priority to meet and greet the pastor of the First Methodist Church in Fort Worth. His name was Tab Wallace - a young, single fellow who loved to hunt. You could say Father loved this trait in the new pastor, while mother thought it was some sinful lust he had. She didn't think a man of the cloth should do any hunting, especially killing.

There was a big, beautiful, Victorian style house just north of town. Mother and Father just fell in love with the place, actually Mother said she liked it better than the home where we had lived in Carterville, Illinois. Father used his hard earned cash and bought it for a song and sung it himself. You see, after selling our house, the store, and the gun shop in Carterville, Father had a good chunk of money to use for rebuilding in Fort Worth.

My father's reputation followed him when he moved to Fort Worth, not as a lawman of any sort; but before we arrived, newspaper articles concerning his fast gun, had migrated out west. He had the trophies to prove it, but certainly not lined up on a shelf in our den at home. Why Mother would have died at the sight! Father kept his trophies at the gun shop where Mother never darkened the door. Oh, she would help out in the hardware store in a pinch. Now, if someone wanted to buy a pistol or rifle, she would refer them to Father. If he wasn't there at the time they could just come back later. She did sell ammunition; it was located in the hardware store.

It was after we moved to Fort Worth that gun sales and repair became a big part of our living. All I had ever known was working in the hardware store after school and on Saturdays. It was a cut and dried thing, when I finished school the business would become mine; course now that was only Father's side of the story. Wouldn't you know, Mother had other plans, which involved going to college and getting a degree in medicine! This may have been the first time Mother and I disagreed. 'Course time would tell, I was only sixteen years-old.

After my family moved and bought the big house in Fort Worth, Texas, we discovered the town sponsored a free "Wild West" performance every Saturday evening right out in Main Street. It always started just as soon as the trail drovers got tanked up at the local saloons around town. As it turned out, the business owners and town folk were getting a bit tired of this foolishness that lasted 'til dawn, most times, especially after several innocent bystanders got shot by stray bullets. Well, push came to shove, and the City Council began to look for another sheriff to replace the one who had managed to get himself shot.

Now don't get ahead of me, but my father's name was brought up many times, and each time my mother 'had a calf'; I'm kidding of course, but you get the picture. My father was elected to the City Council and Mother didn't mind. She seemed to gloat in the publicity that her husband was "sitting in the gate," as she called it, something to do with the Bible, of course.

Personally, as a young boy, I thought it would be great to have Father as the sheriff of a growing town like Fort Worth, Texas. My father's answer was always the same, "I don't need the money, and I don't like getting shot at." He, being a council member, had discussed with every other member that something had to be done about the shooting in the saloons and in the middle of Main Street. Actually this had now become an everyday thing, not just on Saturday night.

Well, my father, along with the other six council members, voted unanimously to run an ad for a sheriff. The advertisement, that Fort Worth was in dire need for a sheriff, was published in the weekly newspaper. 'Course now, the next day after the ad came out in the newspaper, in rode a young cowboy to apply for the sheriff's job. Father said the cowboy was too young and inexperienced for the job, but the others members were grasping for straws, and outvoted Father. Needless to say, the young man needed the money, so he took the job as sheriff of Fort Worth Texas. His name was Jim Branson, and he was from Houston Texas; well...that's what the town put on his tombstone. I've got to admit he looked the part; he wore two Colt peacemakers on his hips and a wide brim hat on his head. It's sad to say, the young man got killed before he drew his first check from the city. As Father said, "We are back at square one," whatever that meant.

You know it's just tear-jerking to say this...but I heard Mother say to her friend in the store one day, that she would pack up and move to another town if the violence continued to get any worse. Well it got worse: it was not only a Saturday performance, but as I earlier said, an' everyday thing. The Chisholm Trail came right through Fort Worth, and naturally this brought travelers from as far away as Mexico. It wasn't just a bunch of cowboys blowing off steam. But the bank of Fort Worth had been robbed twice in the same year; one has to admit this was a little much, to say the least.

The Town Council was hounding Father continuously about taking the job as sheriff. They even agreed to hire two deputies to help him. What was that ol' saying: 'You can catch more flies with honey than you can with vinegar'? I was only sixteen or so when Mother made the final decision for Father to become Sheriff of Fort Worth I remember it well, as if it was yesterday; it was at dinner, course I call it supper.

"Elizabeth is it all right if I invite a special guest over for dinner tomorrow night?"

"Oh yes, William, I don't mind."

"Well, I just thought I would ask, I didn't want to put you out if you had other plans."

"No, I'm free tomorrow night, as far as I know. Could I ask who the special guest is so I will know how, and what to serve?"

"It's the Honorable Edmond J. Davis and his charming wife."

Well, needless to say, Mother was speechless for a second or two.

"You are not talking about the Governor of Texas, are you, William?"

"Yes I am, the one and same, the Governor of Texas, the Lone Star state."

"Now, William, you should have given me more notice than this to plan my menu," Mother said walking back and forth wringing her hands.

"I hear the governor just loves turnips and sow belly."

"Now, William dear, I will prepare the meal and I assure you it will be fit for a king... less turnips greens and sow belly. And Billy, you quit sitting over there laughing, you're getting just like your father here lately."

I must say, as a sixteen year-old boy I knew I was to be seen but not heard; I had my orders. Mother knew how to use a razor strop as well as Father, the only difference, Father sharpened his razor and Mother sharpened my intellect, at least that's what she said. Evidently it was behind me some place. I was old enough to know that the governor was pulling the wool over my mother's eyes; he had come to ask my father to be Sheriff of Fort Worth, but never mentioned the subject during dinner. But he 'shore' did do some bragging; of course his wife wanted to know every recipe and how mother fixed each dish. You might say the Governor and his wife were leading a sheep to slaughter.

'Course now Mother had 'put on the dog'. Dinner was excellent, and I'm not just saying that! Mother even asked a friend to come over and help her serve. Coffee was being served in the front room after dinner when the Governor got down to brass tacks. I was in my room, but left the door open so I could hear every word.

"William, I'm letting you know I am stationing a few federal troops in Fort Worth until we can establish law and order, and get the violence in town under control. I am also going to appoint a U.S.

Marshal to take over. I understand the town will supply two deputies to do most of the work. You will be more than a sheriff, William; you will have mostly paper work and records to keep. I'm asking if I can appoint you as Marshal of Fort Worth County?" It got quiet as a church mouse, and then I heard Father clear his throat.

"Now, Governor Davis, this is so sudden; I think Elizabeth and I should give this some thought."

"No hurry, William, just be sure you bring Elizabeth when you come to the capitol in Austin to be sworn in as U.S. Marshal. We usually have a big shindig; most all the senators and congressman are there."

Well, you might say Mother let stars get in her eyes, and was somewhat hoodwinked, but to make a long story short...Father accepted the position of U.S. Marshal of Fort Worth County...and with Mother's blessing. There was never a gun mentioned throughout the whole process that evening.

During the next two weeks I heard my father saying to one of several men that came into his gun shop, "Ralph, I don't mind telling you, I believe I have bitten off more than I can chew with this marshal job."

"Now, now, William ol' chap, keep a stiff upper lip, it's bound to improve with age, my good man."

"Ralph, we ain't talking about a bottle of wine; we're talking about a damn fool walking around the streets of Fort Worth with a badge pinned to his vest, a target for every gun happy galoot in Texas."

"Now, William, I been knowing you ever since you moved into town and established your hardware store; why, I've been your best customer. And something else, you know I would do anything in the world for you."

"I know it, Ralph, and I appreciate all the business you have brought...Just make sure you keep your black suit pressed."

I know one thing; my father took the job seriously...maybe a little too seriously, at times. For example, Father made a motion to the City Council that he thought that all guns must be checked in at the sheriff's office when anyone hit town - that went over like a fly in the punch bowl. The two deputies, George and Martin, were dumb as a sack of rocks; I heard Father say they didn't know how to get in out of the rain, course he didn't let them know that.

"I'm telling you, Martin, and you too, George, them pistols hanging on you fellows' sides, aren't to drive nails or to beat someone over the head with. You'd better learn to shoot them and learn to fast draw, or you're going to get killed. I'm going ahead and saying it to your face and not to your back... the town of Fort Worth hired you as a joke, and it's up to you to make something of yourselves." I was at the jail house when Father was talking to George and Martin; they were listening to what he had to say but saying very little.

"I'm going to tell you something else," Father said, "if you are to be my deputies, you will start dressing differently. I understand you both are married, so tell your wives to start washing your clothes, and I'll see to it that the city advances you money to buy some decent boots, belts, and a hat."

Well, that got a smile out of the two.

Most times Father worked in his gun shop after the hardware store closed in the evening. I heard him mumbling to himself that this marshal job was taking up more of his time than he thought.

"Father, I heard you tell George and Martin you were going to teach them how to fast draw and shoot a pistol the other day."

"That's right, son...we going to start tomorrow, what about it?" Father said, sitting at his work bench putting a pistol back together.

"I thought maybe you could sorta kill two birds with one rock, and let me kinda follow along and learn with George and Martin."

Father just stopped what he was doing and looked right at me. "You know how your mother feels about you fooling around with guns, son."

I could see in my father's expression the answer to my request was no. He needed more persuading. "I have already been fooling around with pistols, Father. I've turned sixteen, and everyone tells me I'm big for my age. Look how big my hands are!"

"You have nearly gotten grown on me, Billy, and I haven't even noticed, I guess I've been so busy here lately."

"Father, I've been practicing my fast draw every chance I get, you wanna see?"

I could tell my father was somewhat surprised. "Where did you get a gun, son?"

"Oh, I just use any peacemaker I find, but I got my own holster and gun belt, I keep it hid... it's over here under these boxes."

"Okay, Billy, go ahead and put it on and let me see what you got." For a minute I could tell my father was proud of me, it seemed that Father always took me for a mama's boy. Seems Mother and I were always talking about books, college, and doctor stuff, and what she wanted for me.

"I built the gun rigging myself, Father, 'course. I copied your fast draw holster." I went ahead and tied it to my leg. "I'll have to borrow a gun out of the showcase since I don't have one of my own."

"Go ahead, son, get what you've gotten used to, and I tell you what I am going to do, if you can draw and dry fire that Colt peacemaker before this hammer on the floor, the gun is yours."

"Let me get ready, Father," I said, as I made sure my Colt was loose in my holster. I held my hands out by my sides. "Okay, Father, I'm ready."

My father was holding the hammer out in front of him, I watched his hand starting to open. When it did I drew and fanned the Colt three times before the hammer hit the floor.

"My lord, Billy! Where did you learn to do that?...That is the fastest draw I have ever seen, and I'm not just saying that because you're my boy."

"I guess I just inherited it from you, Father."

"Well you got your own Colt peacemaker, son, if that is the one you want. And you'd better not tell your mother either."

"I know what you mean, Father, we would both be in trouble. Can I use real cartridges now?"

"Yes, and I will teach you all I know about hitting what you are shooting at."

I celebrated with a party that Saturday, and had my friends over for cake and punch, but guns were never brought up.

Another whole year passed. I was going on seventeen now, and Mother had never seen me with my gun rigging on. When I would asked Father could I start wearing my Colt, he would just shake his head no.

It just so happened that George and Martin got mighty fast with a gun, but not fast as me. 'Course now, George and Martin weren't gonna tell that to anyone. It hurt their pride...a sixteen year old boy, not even dry behind the ears, could out draw and out shoot faster than grown men. Naturally, Father wasn't gonna let the cat out of the bag either, on account of Mother 'having that calf'; and I don't think I would be kidding much.

In the first half year you might say Father and his two deputies had tamed the town without one man getting killed. Oh, my lord, there was plenty of shooting and fighting; but the wild cowboys around Fort Worth found my father wasn't a pushover when he pulled down on a man in a fair fight. I saw my father actually bend a pistol barrel over several heads rather than shoot to kill. There were more than a couple of men in Fort Worth that couldn't use their right hand for drawing their pistol. My father was so good; he could shoot a gun right out of a man's hand.

Fort Worth had a jail....a big jail, and a good jail....and my father didn't mind putting a man in it until he sobered up. 'Course he would lock one up for fighting or ripping and swearing in, front of the women in the saloon. I saw him...I might need to rephrase that remark I started to make...I wasn't allowed in saloons, but I heard he had no use for a cheating gambler passing through Fort Worth. I do know Father ran more gamblers and gunslingers out of town than you could shake a stick at. They didn't like it, but they knew my father's reputation with a six-gun.

I ain't saying Father didn't have enemies; you could write a book on the men that swore they were gonna get him one day, for one reason or another. I believe Tom Murdock and his cousin Gail Fleming gave my father more trouble than anyone in Fort Worth Texas. According to Father, they were born troublemakers, and he never knew whether to run or duck when he saw them coming.

"I wish your father didn't have to go up to Houston this week; they tell me we are in for some bad weather," Mother said to me as she moved the curtains and looked out the big picture window.

"Mother, you just worry too much nowadays."

"Well, I might do, but I have plenty to worry about," she said turning to face me. "And what is that you're reading? From where I'm standing, it looks like something about guns."

"Well, it is, Mother... it's about Sam Colt...his life story."

I heard Mother huff, then she turned and headed into the kitchen. "I think you would be much more content knowing more about the life stories of Matthew, Mark, Luke and John," she said drily, looking back over her shoulder.

I wanted to cheer Mother up since Father was gone, so I put the book away. I guess she had heard right. Through the window I saw some lightning flashing just south of us, and then the wind began to pick up. It was scary to hear the wind whistling through the high gables and around the corners of this big house.

Mother and I were sitting at the kitchen table eating a bowl of tomato soup with some homemade crackers, when the worst weather came - lightning and thunder - the worst I have ever heard. 'Course I'm not that old now, but it seems as if every new storm is worse than the last.

"I wish your father had waited until later to go to Houston on business."

I guess if I had told her Father had gone to a big gun show, unbeknownst to her, there's no telling what she would have done. The storm was almost unbearable; we could feel the house shake at times, and the lightning was striking so close by that Mother went on into her bedroom. She said she was going to pray, and that I needed to do the same thing before I turned in for the night.

I figured what my mother didn't know wouldn't hurt her. I carried a coal oil lamp to the living room and started back to reading about the life of Samuel Colt, and the guns he had invented. I sat there and read for a couple of hours, and couldn't tell that the weather had let up one bit. It seemed to have grown worse, in some respects.

I put the lamp out and eased on to my room. I carefully slid the book between my mattresses, and finished getting ready for bed. I don't know what time it was, but it was late, and the storm was still raging.

I hadn't for got to pray although I had lot on my mind, I lay there just thing about the big gun show father was at and wished I could of went with him. I was hoping he would bring me a gun-book as a present.

Chapter Two

The Bank Was Robbed Last Night

The next morning was the Lord's Day and it was good daylight before I even woke up. I thought I heard a knock on our front door; I rolled over and trained my ear in that direction to hear if someone was knocking. Evidently Mother had risen before me, because I smelled coffee brewing in the kitchen. I guess by now she had gone to see who was knocking at the front door. I could plainly tell it was George and Martin, my father's two deputies...I quickly put on my slippers and housecoat and went to see what the commotion was all about.

"Billy, I was just asking your ma when Marshal Blunt was coming back from Houston. There's been an emergency over at the bank." Both men was standing there looking as if they had lost their only friend.

"What kind of a emergency are you talking about?" I would have believed anything they said, after that storm last night.

"Well, it's been robbed!"

"Been robbed!" I exclaimed.

"We haven't been over there yet, but that is what Jessie Brooks, the bank president, came to the jailhouse and told us."

Mother said she had something in the oven and went on back in the kitchen. She claimed these were worldly matters, and separated herself from it all.

"Did Mr. Brooks say anything else...how it happened?"

"Billy, that's the one reason we came over here first. Could you get ready and go to the bank with us? We know you stay abreast of your pa's business, and you have a better head on your shoulders than we do...besides, you can give the marshal the facts when he gets back Monday."

I nodded and went to the kitchen where Mother was fixing breakfast. "George and Martin asked me to run over to the bank with them this morning, I'll be right back."

"Don't you forget this is Sunday, and we need to be in church; I just hope our pastor has us a good sermon this morning."

There were limbs and leaves blown all over the place, and a few small trees blown up by the roots, but all in all, the storm had passed and it looked as if we were in store for a sunny day.

The three of us kicked as much mud off of our boots as we could, and knocked on the bank door. It was quickly unlocked by Mr. Brooks.

"Come on in men, it looks really bad... I'm just at rope's end, and speaking of rope, come this way." The three of us followed Mr. Brooks to the back of the bank where a rope was hanging from the ceiling. It was apparent the giant door to the bank vault had been blown open. Traces of explosives still lingered in the air. "As far as I can tell, all of the paper money is gone," Mr. Brooks said, nervously wringing his hands.

"Do you have any idea who might have done this?" I questioned, while George and Martin were looking around for other clues. "You men found anything, besides a new rope hanging out of the ceiling?"

"One more thing - there is a ladder leaning up behind the back of the bank building," George said, coming in the back door of the bank.

"Good! If we find who owns the ladder, we can nab the robbers," Martin quickly explained.

"Let's go over to the general store or the hardware and find out who recently bought a piece of new rope," I said, not thinking about the stores being closed on Sunday.

"One thing for sure, going after them with a posse is out of the question; it would be absolutely impossible with no tracks; the rain washed them out," George said, coming over our way.

I borrowed a pencil and pad from Mr. Brooks. "Now if you will, help me jot down what we know, as of right now, so I can give our findings to my father when he comes in on the train Monday."

George spoke up first, "The way I see it, it was more than one person that did this. I would say the bank was robbed during the lightning and heavy thunder. It stands to reason that the bank vault door was blown open while it was lightning so bad. The ladder was used to climb up on the roof of the bank, a hole was torn in the roof right over the front of the vault; then they stomped a hole in the ceiling, and came down the rope."

"No more than I know, being only sixteen years old, I would say you have a pretty good handle on what went on here last night; I think Father will be proud of his deputies!"

"Mr. Brooks, if you want me to go up in the loft and untie the rope I'll be more than glad to," George offered.

"That will be fine, George. Could you please see what has to be done to fix the roof, while you're up there?"

"Mr. Brooks, I know you go to church on Sunday, but you need to hire someone to fix the roof, now; if it comes another down pour it will damage lots of stuff in the bank," said Martin, looking through the hole in the ceiling and roof.

"Well, what about you and George?" Mr. Brooks asked. "I will pay you good wages, and you can still be on deputies' time."

"What about it up there, George, can we do the job?" George stuck his head down through the ceiling hole. "Yeah, we can do the job Mr. Brooks, but what is going to keep some robber from doing it the second time?"

"That is a good question, George, I will bring it before the bank committee first thing Monday morning...meanwhile, since there is nothing left to steal but loose change, I'm going to leave the keys with you men, and I'm going to church this morning. And Billy, you better do the same, or your mother will skin you alive!"

Mother was huffing and a puffing when I made it back home. I quickly put on my black suit, remembering I hadn't harnessed the horse up to the surrey. By now Mother was fuming; she said she had never been late for church or missed hearing the Word of God preached on a Sunday. Out the back door I ran, and as fast as I could I hitched the horse to the surrey, and met Mother in the front yard; luckily, we made it to church on time. I almost felt sorry for Mother at times; she let everything worry her.

"Just take it with a grain of salt, Mother, don't let it get to you!" I urged.

"I thank you...I don't eat salt, it's not good for my high blood pressure," was her sarcastic reply. You see what I mean?

As she and I eased down from the surrey and started up the cobblestone walk to the church, Mrs. Gertrude Meadows headed our way. "Pardon me Mrs. Blunt, but you have your hat on backwards," she remarked disparagingly.

Well, that was enough to almost put Mother over the edge. Personally, I thought it looked better on backward; I liked the flowers on the back of the hat, myself. Mother quickly regained her composure and let Mrs. Meadows help her straighten her hat. She always said that Mrs. Gertrude was a busy-body, keeping her nose in everybody's affairs.

As usual, Miss Pauline Peterson sat at the organ playing that creepy music; Mr. Craig Watson, the funeral director, hired Pauline to play at funerals. To me, her playing at church sounded as if we were going to bury someone every Sunday. As the song director stepped behind the pulpit ready to open service, Mother leaned over and punched me on the arm gently to get my attention.

"I don't see Pastor Tab Wallace, do you?" Before I could say yea or nay, the song director shed light on mother's question.

"Our Pastor... Reverend Tab Wallace, is not with us this morning, I understand he is away on business in Houston and will be back on tomorrow's train."

I caught mother's gaze, she shrugged her shoulders and twisted her mouth, knowing full well we were going to be bored to death by Mr. Harget, our Adult Sunday School teacher. He was long-winded, with no end to his sermons. Someone said a lady approached Brother Harget after he had preached a three point sermon one Sunday morning: 'Brother Harget, I have three points I would like to make!' she said with a sinister attitude. 'Brother Harget, number one, you read your whole sermon…number two… you don't read all that well, and number three, it wasn't worth reading in the first place.' They said she never darkened the door of our church again.

I started to tell Mother about our pastor coming in the gun shop Friday and talking to Father about the goings on this weekend at the Annual Knife and Gun Show in Houston. I could just see Father and our pastor, in my subconscious, having a good breakfast at one of them swanky up-town restaurants in Houston. Then they would be on their way over to the Annual Knife and Gun Show to have a wonderful time looking at guns of all kinds: antique, as well as modern.

I sat there thinking about what I'd read during the storm last night…(and I guess I shouldn't bet in the church, but, I'd bet if Mr. Colt had been alive he would have been there at that big gun show)… Samuel Colt had been born July 19, 1814 and died January 10, 1862. He was an American inventor and industrialist. The book had said this about him: 'He was the founder of Colt's Patent Fire-Arms Manufacturing Company (now known as Colt's Manufacturing Company), and was widely credited with popularizing the revolver. Colt's innovative contributions to the weapons industry have been described by arms historian, James E. Serven, as events which shaped the destiny of American Firearms.'

While daydreaming about Mr. Colt and the Houston gun show, all of a sudden I felt a sharp pain in my left side; I swallowed several times real hard….praying it wasn't appendicitis….or something even worse. I glanced at Mother just as the pain struck again; it was her elbow.

"Where is your mind, Billy? And you are mumbling to yourself… why your mind seems to be a thousand miles from here," Mother whispered in my ear.

"It's not that far to Houston, Mother," I whispered back.

By the time Mr. Harget finished his morning message all of our guts were growling; I'm sure Mother would have put it another way. I was hungry. It was nearly one o'clock. I guess I took after my mother on some things, for instance, my impression of Mr. Harget's talk this morning. His text was from I Samuel 15:33, where all the people brought the sheep and cattle, as well as King Agag, back to King Saul. The Bible says the prophet, Samuel, took a sword and hewed him to pieces. Mother said on the way home from church that his talk had made her sick to her stomach. Personally, I don't believe she had fully recovered from being caught wearing her hat backwards.

The next morning George Simmons, Martin Travick, and I were at the train depot to meet and greet Father. It was for sure we would be bending his ear. We all had a story to tell about Saturday night's stormy bank robbery. We also had a visitor at the jailhouse when the four of us rode up.

"My name is Gladys Murdock, and I want to report a missing person," the visitor announced.

"Well, Miss Murdock, why don't you sit right over here and tell me all about it," Marshal Blunt encouraged..

"I'm also mad!" she continued.

"There's not much we can do about you being mad, but we are pretty good at finding missing persons. Just tell us who it is; and how long this person has been missing?"

"Marshal, it's my husband, Tom, he loaded up Saturday evening and left home, and I ain't seen e'm since."

"You say he loaded up; are you saying he packed a grip and walked out the door?"

"Oh no, as far as I know he didn't carry any clothes, Marshal."

I could tell there was more to this story.

"Didn't you think it was strange, your husband leaving home and not carrying his clothes?" questioned the marshal.

"Not really, I was talking about him packing up his buckboard with his tools, you know he does odd jobs around town."

"Okay, I get it now, you thought he was going to work, but he never came back home."

"Marshal! I knew he wasn't going to work; it was too late; and the weather was getting bad and seemed to be getting worse by the minute. He and Gail Fleming has been settin' around all week talking about going to California 'when their ship came in'. I thought they might find a ship in California, but you and I both know there ain't no ships in Fort Worth."

"Let me get this straight now, Mrs. Murdock, you see, I just came in from a trip to Houston and haven't even been home yet. You say he went out in the bad weather and loaded up his tools and drove off, and you haven't seen hair nor hide of him since?"

"Father, ask her if he had a ladder on the wagon when he drove off." As I spoke, Mrs. Murdock looked up and caught my gaze.

"Oh, yes, he carries that dumb ladder every where he goes, he works on lots of roofs, you know."

"Is there anything else that we should know that might speed up the process of finding him?"

"Well, I did swing by Mrs. Fleming's house before I came here. That's Gail's ma... She said Gail hadn't been home either, but that wasn't surprising. So I would say wherever you find one, you will find the other."

"Mrs. Murdock, maybe you haven't heard yet, but the bank was robbed Saturday night during all that bad weather. According to George, my deputy, that piece of rope he is holding there in his hand was bought by your husband from Mr. Watson over at the general store. It was used in the robbery."

"I can tell y'all right now, I don't know nothing about no rope or robbery! Besides, Tom Murdock is not my husband; he never did marry me. That's right; I've been shacking up with that bum for nearly two years. He said he was gonna carry me to California when he went." You could tell Mrs. Murdock was upset.

"Then you're sure he has struck a trot to California?"

"Just as sure as I can be, and I'm positive that Gail Fleming is right along with him."

"Mrs. Murdock, you've been a big help, there is only one main road to California from here, and I imagine our bank robbers will take that course. With them traveling in a buckboard, and me and Martin on horseback, we will probably apprehend them before they get out of the state of Texas; besides, they still have to go through New Mexico and Arizona before getting to California."

"Marshal, I hope you get 'em, I'll be over at the diner working, if I can help with anything else."

"Martin, you and George saddle us two good horses, and two spares to carry with us, then go by the general store and pack us plenty of food to carry with us; no telling when we'll be back. Mr. Gene Watson knows what we need. Whatever you do, don't forget to pack a skillet, a coffee pot, and two mugs."

I was sure hoping my father would let me go with them. "Father, what would be the chances of you letting me go with you all on this little mission? You may need another gun."

"I'd sure like to, son, but I'm already in the doghouse with your mother for running off Saturday and Sunday; and now I'm taking off again. Suppose you and George take care of Fort Worth, while me and Martin go looking for the bad men."

"Does that mean I can spend time here in the jail?"

"I guess so, but let's not make your mother mad with us, no worse than she already is."

"By the way, Father, I received the gun book I ordered from New York, and I've been reading it at night. I was sure hoping you could tell me what all you saw and did at the gun and knife Show."

"Well, come on and walk with me over to the bank; I need to see Jessie Brooks before I leave. And then I must go by the house to see your mother before I head out after the bank robbers."

By the time Father finished talking to Mother, who wasn't in a good mood about him running off again, Martin was at the house, with the horses saddled and ready to ride. I said goodbye to Father, and watched him ride away.

I was sixteen and I had been reading books about law and order that detailed the worst outlaws and famous law men of the wild, wild, west. I knew the hazards of being a lawman like my father, and I could understand my mother's concern - would Father get killed, or would he bring the robbers back to Fort Worth for trial?

I'll let Father share this account in his own words. . .

I guess Martin and I were a few miles from town heading due west. In that short time we had the horses trained to follow instead of trying to get ahead of us.

"Martin have you ever killed a man before?" I asked, looking over his way.

"No sir, Marshal, but I've seen some folks I'd like to kill; and I've seen some folks that needed a good killing. Why do you ask?"

"In the first place, Martin, the reason I chose you to go on this mission with me - it seems you have more grit in your craw than George. I wouldn't want that to get back to him, if you know what I mean."

"I know what you mean, Marshal, you had rather have me backing you up in a gun fight than George."

"I believe you hit the nail right on the head, Martin, I have watched you both shoot... I think you are faster and more apt to hit your target."

"Marshal, I appreciate you saying that, and having that much confidence in me. As you know, I ain't never been much, we were just poor folks; some even called my ma and pa 'white trash'. As I look back now, I guess the apple don't fall too far from the tree."

"I think you and George are trying to make something out of your lives, and personally, I think the town of Fort Worth is taking notice."

We rode on and talked about every subject Martin knew.

Watching the sun go down, I asked, "Don't you think we need to pull up for the night? We can get an early start in the morning."

"I think you're right, Marshal, I need some daylight to fix us some supper."

"I'll rustle us up some wood and get a fire going while you dig out that coffee pot I hope you brought with us. By the time Martin and I finished supper, if it hadn't been for the campfire we could not have seen our hands in front of our faces. We had tied our horses in some good grass, and they were happy. Another good thing was that a small stream ran right next to our camp. By the looks of things we had the Lone Star State all to ourselves; no one passed us going or coming. One thing about it, I had brought someone with me that knew how to cook.

"Where did you learn to cook like this, Marvin?" I asked, as I reached for seconds of biscuits and brown gravy.

"Well, Ma never had any girls, so I had to do all the kitchen chores, and just learned by trial and error."

"It sure was good, Marvin, I might have eaten too much, but I think now I'll make it 'til morning. I don't know this country all that well, but we should reach the town of Albany tomorrow."

"Well, if I know Tom Murdock, with all that money he has, if there is a saloon in this town, we'll probably find him sooner than we think."

"I say the sooner the better, I got other things to do besides spending my time riding all over the country side looking for bank robbers."

Chapter Three

Catching The Crooks

Sure enough Marvin and I rode into Albany, Texas about two o'clock in the afternoon. We tied our mounts to the hitching post and went straight to the saloon. As we started across the street something just told me to pull off my badge and put it in my pocket.

"What are you doing, Marshal?"

"Something in my spirit just told me to take off my badge, and I suggest you do the same thing," I replied.

Now it being early, and on a week day, the saloon was almost empty.

"You want a beer?" I asked, walking up to the bar.

"Might as well, if you are buying."

"Gimmy two beers and some information," I said to the friendly bartender who looked as if he enjoyed his job.

"Two beers coming up, but the information around here sometimes is a little sketchy," said the bartender, doing an about face with two beer mugs in his hand.

"What do you mean, 'sometimes the information is a little sketchy'?" I asked, as the bartender served us.

A smile came across his face as he replied, "One lives a lot longer that way. What did you fellers want to know, how far is it to the next town, or do I own a horse?"

"Neither, we're looking for two cousins that left Fort Worth sometime Saturday, heading for California. To make a long story short, their mother died Sunday morning, leaving them a small fortune in the Fort Worth Bank."

The bartender began to shine a shot glass while I was talking. "I don't reckon I would get in any trouble if I helped a good cause." He picked up another shot glass and went on with his story. "There were two strangers in here Sunday night, dressed fit to be killed in all new duds, said they had come into a fortune. They started buying drinks for everyone. 'Course now, it being Sunday night and all, the usual crowd was down. You don't suppose they could be your men, do you?"

The bartender didn't know it, but his story was fitting right into my lie about the two cousins and their dead mother. "Oh, well now, they were already rich; they knew their mother was going to leave them a fortune when she died."

"In other words; the two men are headed for California and don't even know their mother is dead?"

"That pretty much sums it up; we are distant relatives and just trying to do the family a favor," I said, looking over at Martin. He just rolled his eyes and finished his beer.

"Well now, gentlemen, you need to talk to Rose Lee, she should be down in a few minutes; she is the star attraction around here. You want another beer while you are waiting?"

I looked back at Martin who answered, "I'm just following the leader, boss man."

I turned to the bartender and barked out, "Two more beers."

By this time the night crowd was wandering in. Martin and I took a table and nursed our beers while we waited on Rose Lee to make her grand appearance.

The wait wasn't that long, Martin and I still had a half glass of beer each. The crowd began to applaud as Rose Lee started down the winding stairs from her room. She smiled at the onlookers, waved her neck wrap, and sashayed to the end of the hardwood bar, where she already had the bartender's attention. Ours included, every eye was glued on Rose Lee. She was wearing a beautiful, long, red dress, very tight fitting, and split down the front. I watched as the bartender poured her a shot of whiskey and made conversation for a few minutes. She swigged the shot down and started for our table, her hips swinging back and forth like the pendulum on a Grandfather Clock. She softly touched the face of every man as she passed their tables.

"Fred tells me you have been waiting for me," she cooed, propping her beautiful high-heeled shoe in an empty chair at our table, completely exposing her red-tinted-silk hosed leg.

"What can you tell us about the two strangers that were in here last night?" I asked, trying to keep my eyes focused on her face.

"Oh yes, what is that ol' cliché: 'a fool and his money is soon parted.' They were spending money like it was growing on cactus bushes. They took two of our high priced girls up to a room and paid them double for their services. And I tell you something else, if you find your friends with their throats slit from ear to ear it wouldn't surprise me one bit."

"Why would you say a thing like that?"

"Simple, they kept telling how much money they had, and how they were on their way to California. Let me tell you...there are men in this town that will cut your throat for less than ten dollars."

"Do you know when they left town?"

"I think when they came back downstairs they said they were going over to the Albany Hotel to spend the night."

I sat my mug down, and said to her as I stood up, "I thank you very much for your help, and I wish we could stay for your act; but we need to get the word to Tom and Gail about their poor, dead mother." The bat wings flopped several times behind us as Martin and I stepped off the boardwalk and started over to the hotel.

"While we're this close, why don't you swing by and check on our horses, then come on over to the hotel," I suggested to Martin. I then walked on over to the hotel.

A guest book and a bell were on the counter at the foot of the stairs, but I saw no clerk. I took up the bell, gave it a couple of jolts and waited. I heard the hinges squeak on a door to the left of me, and looked around. There stood a man in his late thirties who looked like he had been in a bare-knuckle, fist fight, with his hands tied behind him.

"Can I help you, sir?" he asked, stepping behind the counter, holding a bloody rag to his nose.

"I might could ask the same question; for Pete's sake, what happened to you, man, you get thrown out of your own hotel?"

"Not hardly, the man in Room Five upstairs won't leave, or pay his bill."

"Oh well... I need to find out if Tom Murdock and Gail Fleming stayed the night in this hotel last night." I noticed the clerk looked a bit dubious about answering the question.

"Sir, you know that it is against the house rules, and unlawful, for me to give out any information pertaining to our guests."

I reached in my pocket, retrieved my marshal badge, and slammed it down on the counter right in front of the clerk. "I am the law!" I practically yelled.

The clerk jumped as if he had been shot, and his eyes got big as saucers. "You really a U. S. Marshal?" he asked, after swallowing a time or two, "maybe you could help me with that bad man in room number five upstairs."

I saw Martin coming through the big glass doors of the hotel and answered, "I'd be more than glad to help you out, here is the man for the job coming in right now."

"Did I hear my name mentioned?" Martin asked, propping his elbow on the counter.

"Yes, the hotel clerk needs an errand run. Go upstairs and tell the man in Room Five it's time to check out, and he can pay as he comes by the desk."

Without any deliberation Martin turned and started up the stairs. It just so happened that Room Five was practically right overhead where we were standing. Now we couldn't hear what was said, but a noise ensued that sounded like a fully-grown horse being castrated, without near enough help to hold the animal down to do the proper job.

The hotel clerk and I trained our eyes on the top of the stairs where two men appeared. Martin, my deputy, was behind a man toting a suitcase. Just as they reached the top step, Martin gave the suitcase a heave, and down the steps it tumbled. Then Martin gave the man a swift kick in the behind, and end over end he followed his luggage, to the bottom floor. The man got up, unfolded himself, put on his hat, grabbed his suitcase, and limped up to the checkout desk.

"That will be six dollars, sir," the clerk said, watching as the man counted out the right currency on the counter. We three stared as the man hobbled to the hotel front door.

"Martin, you could have hurt that man, the way you kicked him down the stairs," I said, trying to keep from laughing.

"You ought to seen what he tried to do me upstairs. I gently tapped on the door to Room Five, and a voice inside said, 'Come in', so I opened the door and stepped inside the room; now this may be hard for y'all to believe, but like a charging bull, here he came toward me, cursing with every breath."

"Oh, I believe you!" exclaimed the hotel clerk.

"Well, I sidestepped the mad man and he hit the wall; I ran to the other side of the room to get away from the fool, and here he came again. I hadn't even told him what you had said yet. Now, Marshal, I haven't ever told you this, but I don't handle rejection well; it's my only vice. I have been this way since childhood; when someone tries to hurt me I go crazy...I become like a deranged, wild, animal. Well, I busted everything in that room over the man's head; and from his bended knees he begged me not to hit him again, promising that he was going to leave."

I took a deep breath, "Well, remind me not to ever make you mad." I looked over at the hotel clerk, "Now what about Tom Murdock and Gail Fleming, did they stay in this hotel last night or not?"

The clerk quickly turned his guest book around so I could see it.

"Right on the bottom of the page, Marshal, Tom Murdock and Gail Fleming, but they are done gone...they wanted to know when the west bound stagecoach would run."

"Do you remember them saying anything about going to California?"

"Yes, they did, Marshal, several times they mentioned California."

I thanked the hotel clerk for the information and Martin apologized for the damage in Room Five. He and I headed over to the stage depot. The stage depot, livery stable, and blacksmith shop were all under one roof, and kept up and owned by the same man. I guess you are wondering how I knew all of this - being the first time I had ever been in this town. It's simple; a large sign, painted across the front of the building read: 'Big John's Livery Stable', and painted in small letters, on the glass door I was about to go in, I read: 'Big John—Owner and Operator'. The shirtless man, standing over by a big anvil,, would have made two of Marvin.

"I take it you are Big John," I remarked.

He laid his hammer down, walked over to a water bucket, and responded, "I presume you are looking for some information." He reached and retrieved a blue granite dipper from its nail, near the wooden bucket.

"Now, how did you know who I was, Big John, since I've never been in this town?" I asked. I looked at Martin, who had a dumbfounded look on his face.

"No, you've never been here, but I was at the capital the night our honorable governor swore you in as U.S. Marshal of Fort Worth, Texas. I was there to negotiate and sign a new contract for the stagecoach line in North Texas."

"I remember seeing you now. Me and my deputy are on the trail of two bank robbers. We got wind through the grapevine that they may have caught the stage going west this morning."

Big John hung the dipper back on the nail, placed his hands on his hips and asked, "What did these two men look like?"

"They are in their early thirties, wouldn't you say so, Martin?" Martin came to attention somewhat and moved closer to where we were. "And they were all dressed up with new clothes: boots, hats, and all."

"That's them...got on the stage right here just awhile ago, I believe if you took a good whiff of air you could still smell the perfume they were wearing. Seems they were all hyped up about going to California."

Martin caught my gaze, nodded, and said, "That's our men, Marshal!"

"The stage will stop at Mill Pond Road, about twenty miles due west from here," Big John explained.

"Oh, by the way...were they carrying any luggage?" I asked.

"Yes, they were, both of them were carrying an extra big, leather suitcase and a regular grip. One thing now makes sense."

"How is that, Big John?" I asked.

"Well, I noticed the luggage was tied with a rope in a hard, fast knot; I just took for granted the locks were broken on the luggage. One other thing, there was a woman passenger on board."

"Do you think she knew the robbers?" I asked.

"I don't believe so; she came by yesterday checking on the departure time of today's stage."

"I do appreciate all the information, Big John, I think Martin and I are going to water the horses, and head west."

"You may catch the stage before it reaches Mill Pond Road; the trail is a little rough, and I trained a new driver on this run. He had worked for the stage line before, but he came by last night wanting a job, and caught us short handed...so I put him on."

There was a wind-mill and a big water trough in the middle of town - very handy for passersby and town folk. Well, we took advantage of the free facilities of the town of Albany, mounted up, and headed west, hoping to catch up with the stage soon. I guess we had been in the saddle pushing pretty hard the better part of three hours, when Martin came up with a hard-to-answer question.

"Marshal, you know Tom Murdock and Gail Fleming know both of us... have you thought what may occur when we catch the stage and have the driver stop?"

"I would say you have a good point, Martin, these two birds are sitting inside the stage and we're outside, sitting on our horses in broad daylight - an open target, if you ask me."

"Do you have a plan?" Martin asked.

"We could pull our bandannas over our faces and make out like we're robbing the stage."

"I'm afraid we might get shot by the driver." Martin said, laughing.

"Well, we better think of something fast, there goes the stagecoach."

We both stopped about the same time, to make our plan to keep from getting shot.

As we sat there discussing what we were going to do, Martin said, "Marshal, I believe the stage is settin' still, don't you have a telescope?"

I reached in my saddlebag and handed Martin my telescope; he quickly extended it, placing it to his eye. I waited and waited. "Well what do you see?" I finally asked Martin, as he kept fumbling with the long, brass telescope.

"Marshal, what I'm looking at I don't think you want to see."

"Give me the glass! I'll look for myself."

Martin just sank in the saddle as he handed me the telescope. I brought the stage into focus.

"You're right, Martin, I'm afraid this complicates matters."

I closed up the telescope, placed it in my saddle bag, and started on down the road to where the stage was sitting, right in the middle of the dusty road.

"One thing about it, Marshal, dead men can't shoot back."

Both Gail Fleming and Tom Murdock lay beside the stage: side by side, shot dead, their pistols still in their holsters.

"See if you can find the driver," I instructed Martin, as we dismounted.

"What was that?" Martin questioned, looking toward the stage.

"What was what?" I asked. As I drew my Colt and slowly moved to the stage I could hear some sniffling inside. I had momentarily forgotten Big John saying there was a female on board. I turned the door handle and gave the door a tug. As it came open there she sat, a beautiful, young lady, scared half to death.

"You need not be afraid now, miss, I'm a U.S. Marshal, and this is my deputy, Martin Travick. You think you may be up to telling us what happened here?"

As I gave her a hand, the young lady climbed out of the stage and asked, "Do either of you have some water?"

Martin was quick to oblige, dashing for his canteen and offering it to her. She took several swigs and handed the canteen back to him.

"First of all, the trip has been very rough to say the least, and the two men, lying there on the ground, were perfect gentleman. All they talked about was how rich they were and how they couldn't wait to get to California," she paused to catch her breath and leaned back against the stage, then continued, "As far as I am concerned, the two on the ground had nothing to do with the stage robbery."

Martin looked at me as if to say, 'you reap what you sow'.

"As I said before, we were riding along and the stage began to slow down; soon it just stopped and the driver got down and walked around the side of the stage. By this time, the two that are lying there dead jumped out of the stage to see what the hold up was. Well, lo and behold, the driver drew his pistol and shot both men dead - point blank. I watched as two men came riding down out of the rocks, leading a horse. I guess, by the looks of things, all they wanted were the two big suitcases the dead men had with them. As far as I know, that is all they took with them when they rode off."

"In other words, the driver did the killing and rode off with the two that brought an extra horse?"

"That's right, the two that brought the spare horse were masked so I couldn't see their faces."

"Did you hear them say anything?" I questioned.

"Not really, although one of the men said something about the border. I think they had this planned ahead of time."

"That figures, they are going to Mexico. Martin, if you will, help me load the two corpses in the stage. We will try to make it on to Mill Pond Road before dark. By the way, miss, do you ride? If you do, you can ride my horse, and you won't have to ride in the stage with the dead bodies."

"I ride very well, thank you, and my name is Blanch Baldwin."

"Martin, if you and Miss Blanch will ride on up ahead you won't be eating the dust from the stage coach."

It wasn't long until we passed the marker: Mill Pond Road - 1 mile. Now, what I saw when I brought the stage into town, was a typical western town, a relay stage stop; that's about all it had going for it. 'Course now, about a good rock's throw on up the street was a board and batten shack. It looked as if a good wind could disarrange its whereabouts within a moment's notice. We explained to the custodian of the relay station what had happened back up the road, and that the corpses were in the stage. When Martin and myself loaded the bodies in the stage we searched their pockets; they had over a thousand dollars between the both of them. I told Martin it was all bank money, and would be returned as soon as he and I returned to Fort Worth.

It's a shame I thought, how a man could be temped, especially a law man. If I ever wanted to go wrong and become rich, now was the time. How would anyone ever know what I skimmed off the top, or what I took from the bank robbery that no one would ever know?

Chapter Four

Our Work Had Just Began

Naturally the stage attendant was glad to get back the stage in one piece, and the team of horses unharmed. He told us that three men had ridden in earlier, and as far as he knew they were still up at the shack, which served as the town's saloon. He also said he recognized one of the men, and thought he had worked for the stage line in the past.

"Miss Blanch, it looks like you are between a rock and a hard place; the relay manager says we don't have a driver to carry the stage on to the next town, which is about thirty miles from here."

"And it looks as if there isn't any place for me to stay until this is all settled," Blanch said, eying the surroundings.

"Well, I hope to get some of it settled in a few minutes, if the three men that rode in here earlier are still up the street at that so-called saloon," I remarked.

"Marshal, there are four horses tied up outside at the hitching rail, do you suppose the men are still there?"

"Let me get astraddle of my horse and we'll find out," I answered.

As Martin and I rode up to the makeshift saloon, we found it quiet as a church mouse. There were three horses tied up outside. It looked as if they had been ridden hard.

"I believe our men are inside, don't you, Marshal? Do you have a plan, other than you and I just kick the front door off the hinges and walk in shooting?" Martin queried.

"I don't know, Martin, is that the best path of wisdom right now, you think?"

"I'm asking you, Marshal, I'm just here for the ride; what do I know?"

I thought for a moment and remembered that neither I nor my deputies had ever been in a situation just like this before. I guess this is what they call: 'where the buck stops'.

"Martin, I was daydreaming and thinking at the same time...you head around to the back door and go in, and I'll come in the front door."

"Splendid idea, Marshal...we're inside now...what do we do?"

"I see what you mean, maybe kicking the door off the hinges isn't such a bad idea after all. Let's go with the back door and front door plan, and just hope they don't recognize us. I'll walk in, go up to the bar and order a drink, then I'll size the situation up. You come in the back door and give me cover, if the shooting starts." I flipped the thong off both my Colts, and made sure they were loose in my holster...as I watched Martin walk around the building. And I was hoping the saloon had a back door.

Now you talking about the blind leading the blind...I was going to walk into this place not knowing who was who; as far as I knew I had never laid eyes on either of the three men. This saloon didn't have bat-wings for doors, but a crudely fashioned thing that resembled a barn door. I made sure I gave Martin plenty of time to get inside before I made my move. As I opened the door and stepped inside, I had only a split second to make my evaluation of the place and come up with a game plan.

The room had no windows; it was dark and musky smelling. The boarded floor squeaked as I walked toward the bar. There were three men sitting together at a table across the room, and an old man with a beard sitting alone at the end of the bar, playing solitaire. As far as I could tell the three men never gave me much thought as I approached the bar, 'course as I said, it was dark. The bearded old man saw I was headed to the bar. Somehow, having sense enough to put two and two together, he eased up from his seat and stepped behind the makeshift bar.

"What's your pleasure, mister?" the old man asked, as he placed both hands on the bar and gave me the once over.

"Whiskey will be fine." I saw Martin walk in the already open back door. The barkeep poured me a hefty drink, and turned his attention to Martin who had just walked up to the other end of the bar. I nonchalantly turned around, letting my back rest on the bar as I downed my shot. I noticed that one of the men across the room looked up, and when he saw Martin, said something to the man sitting beside him At this point they all looked up, as if they might have known him from Fort Worth.

But, what really caught my attention were the two huge suitcases tied up with rope, sitting behind them, against the wall. Well, it was for sure we had our men, but which of the three was the stage coach driver? What difference did it make now? They were all going to be arrested, or shot; it was up to them. I set my shot glass on the bar behind me and started toward their table. All the men had their hands where I could see them.

"Which one of you works for the stage coach line?" I inquired.

As if by habit... two of the men turned and looked at the older, red-faced man with a beer gut.

"Who wants to know?" asked the overweight man, as he slid his chair back from the table, and dropped his hand onto his pistol butt.

"I wouldn't do that if I were you, mister, I'm a U. S. Marshal from Fort Worth, and the fastest gun in this part of Texas."

Now either he didn't believe me, or he wasn't planning on going back to Fort Worth to stand trial for murder. When he stood up, he literally shoved his chair across the floor at me and went for his pistol; that was the second mistake he had made today. As the big man touched his pistol and started to take it out of the holster, I drew and fanned a slug aimed at his pistol butt; the pistol exploded in his hand and blood flew as his pistol sailed across the room. With blood still dripping, he caught his hand in surprise; you could see the pain in his face. By this time, Martin had joined the crowd and had his pistol drawn on the other two.

"I'm arresting you three for the murder of Tom Murdock and Gail Fleming."

"Now, just a minute, Marshal, we had nothing to do with the killing," one of the younger men stated, begging off.

"That's right, Marshal," the other young man explained, "it was all Hector's doing; we told him we didn't have to kill Tom and Gail, they were kin folks of ours."

"Take their guns, Martin, they got a long ride ahead of them."

I cuffed them with the extra hand-cuffs in my saddle bag; then we all rode back to the stage depot where the stage and the young lady were.

"Is this the stage driver and the man who shot the two men that were on the stage from Albany with you this morning?" I asked Blanch, as the men dismounted. I brought the one they called Hector around, so she could get a good look.

"That's him, Marshal, that's the man that shot the two men on the stage...and the other two are the men who brought the extra horse for him," she replied, pointing toward them.

Major Ellis, the stage coach attendant at this relay station, came out to where we were all standing. We were trying to make a decision as to how we could best get the prisoners to jail in Fort Worth.

"The wife came by earlier and got acquainted with Miss Blanch. She plans for her to stay with us until the westbound stage comes tomorrow," Major Ellis explained.

"That's right neighborly of you and your wife, Major, this takes a burden off my hands. I would like to commandeer the stagecoach to take the prisoners back to Fort Worth. Is there any way you can get Tom Murdock and Gail Fleming buried? I will pay the charge, if you can find someone to dig their grave in boot hill."

Martin and I unloaded the two bodies at the relay station and had the three prisoners to board the stage, making sure they were hand-cuffed. We made sure the two suitcases were securely tied on the top of the stage, as well. Martin tied our horses to the back of the stage, hoping they wouldn't be any trouble on the trip. He and I climbed on the driver's box, and 'come hell or high water' we were on our way back to

Fort Worth. But what we didn't know...we would face 'hell and high water' in the next few days before reaching Fort Worth

I hope you don't think I was prophesying when I referred to hell or high water...but before we reached Albany, there came a flood upstream on the Fowler River - breaking the ferry loose, and washing it no telling how far downstream. So there we sat on the bank with nothing to eat, and it looked like more rain on the way. There was one thing for sure, there was no way to get the stage across the river in the next week, especially if it kept on raining.

"What do you think, Martin?" I asked, as he and I stood on the bank of the Fowler River watching the raging tide.

"It's hopeless, if you are asking me. We still have five horses tied behind the stage. But don't you think the river is too swift, even for a good quarter horse to swim?"

"Well, if push comes to shove, I alone would try it; but we have three prisoners to look out for." I answered, walking back to the stage coach where the prisoners were sitting.

"That's right, and we have two suitcases containing no telling how much money; and you and I certainly can't afford losing it, or our trip would be in vain, don't you think, Marshal?"

"Martin, I was just thinking, do you remember that ranch house on the right side of the road, just before we came to the river?"

Martin was checking the team horses over making sure the harness was intact. "Yes, I do, what about it?"

"For one thing, we could go back there and maybe buy some food...ain't you getting hungry?"

"Yes, I am, but I didn't want to say anything, I've never been one to complain." Martin rubbed his belly.

"Me neither, but I do make a few exceptions when I'm starving to death, and I don't think these low life scum sitting in the stage are worth you and me starving over!" I exclaimed, taking on an attitude. "Let's turn this stage around and go back to that ranch house we saw a ways back; we might make it before dark."

As we started down the lane toward the ranch house the stagecoach caused quite a stir; evidently the rancher's pack of dogs wasn't accustomed to having a stage coach pull up to their front gate. Neither was the rancher; he appeared at the front door of the ranch house with a rifle. We just sat there as he began scolding the dogs; one by one they hushed and went back under the house.

"You fellows lost, or having problems?" the rather tall man asked. He walked to the edge of the porch, still holding the rifle on us.

"We ain't lost...but we are sure having some problems. I'm William Blunt, U. S. Marshal from Fort Worth, and this is Deputy Martin Travick. The three men inside the stage are our prisoners; they have killed two men and we are taking them back to Fort Worth to stand trial."

The rancher lowered the rifle and walked out to the gate. "And the river is out of its banks and the ferry is nowhere to be found," he commented, as a woman appeared in the doorway beside him.

"You pretty well hit the nail on the head, sir, and we were just wondering if you could give us lodging in your barn for the night... it looks like the rain is coming this way again."

"Who is it, Phil?" the woman asked, as she walked onto the porch.

"It's the marshal from Fort Worth, with a load of prisoners." He paused and turned toward her. "It's all right, Maggie, you can go on back in the house."

The woman stood still for a moment, then turned to go back in the house. I quickly thought this was the time to kill two birds with one stone.

"Sir, I believe your wife called you Phil, do you mind if I ask a favor of your wife?"

The woman quickly stopped and looked back at me as I started getting down off the stagecoach.

"I know it's late ma'am, and I'm sure you're tired from the day's chores, but if your husband, don't mind, I have a thousand dollars to buy some food, I'll give you part, half, or all of it to fix vittles for us and the prisoners, until the river goes down and we can cross."

The woman looked at her husband, and replied, "I don't mind. It's up to my husband, we sure could use the money right now."

"As I said, ma'am, you will be well reimbursed for your food and labor, and Phil, we will pay you for the use of your barn. If you will let our horses graze on your pasture while we're here, you will be well compensated."

"I think that request can be granted, Marshal. As my wife said, she and I sure could use the money right now. It is our son, he needs surgery; and we must carry him to Houston to get a specialist to perform the operation."

"I can say one thing, you folks will be well paid, and never forgotten, and listen Mrs. Maggie... please...we don't need nothing fancy; so don't deprive yourself or the boy."

Phil walked back to his wife, handed her the rifle, and motioned Martin to take the stage on down to the barn. By this time it had begun to lightly sprinkle.

"You men, go ahead and get out of the stage and go into the barn. Hay will be your mattress until the river goes down enough for us to cross." I borrowed a piece of chain from Phil and he rounded up a good, heavy-duty padlock. He and I quickly made a secure configuration by doubling the chain around a post in the barn, then through their hand-cuffs. One thing for sure, this is where they would stay. 'Course, they had enough slack to use the bathroom in the corner of the barn.

Martin had unsaddled the horses, and thrown the saddles, blankets, and the harness for the team into the empty stage, using it for storage. It looked as if the horses were glad to be free and on some green grass. I caught Phil's gaze and asked if he had any room in the ranch house for the two suitcases we had taken off the top of the stage. Of course, he had no idea what was in them, at the time. I did a double-take on our prisoners, making sure they were settled in and as comfortable as they could be - under the circumstances - being hand-cuffed to a heavy chain locked to a six by six-inch barn-support. At least they had plenty of fresh hay to sleep on.

"I'll have you men some food down here in a few minutes," I explained, as I looked all around, to make certain there weren't any pitchforks, or other type of tools, in reaching distance of these polecats.

"Marshal, you had ought to turn me and Darby loose; we didn't do nothing!"

"Didn't do anything, my butt, you two were willing to rob your own kinfolk!"

"Well, it wasn't their money," the young man replied.

"And what makes you think it was your money in the first place? How did you two get the stage driver involved in your thieving scheme?" I asked. The raindrops were now falling heavily onto the tin roof. Phil Coker and Martin came running in out of the rain, after turning the horses out to pasture.

"I believe its set in for the night, Marshal, you can ask Phil."

"It could be, but I'm no authority on the weather; it pretty much does what it wants to do," commented Phil, "Oh well, if it slacks up for one minute you fellows run on up to the house. Maggie should have you and your deputy some supper fixed."

"You and your wife are being very kind, helping us out like this. We were really between a rock and a hard place, if you know what I mean," I said to Mr. Coker.

"Marshal, me and my wife Maggie have been through that rock and hard place you speak of; she and I had two boys. The son that needs the operation is almost paralyzed, and Jerry, the other son, is just a step ahead of the law." He hung his head. "The wife and I have spent a small fortune just keeping him out of prison here lately."

"Where is Jerry now?" I asked.

"Who knows? He comes and goes as he wants to; sad to say, I gave up on him long ago."

"What about your wife?" I asked.

"She hasn't given up like I have; she prays for the boy every night, that he will change. It looks like the rain has slacked off; let's try to make it to the house before the bottom falls out again."

Without any more prodding, Martin, with one suitcase, and me with the other, tore out toward the back porch of the ranch house. 'Course Mr. Coker, not having a load to carry, led the way.

"Now, if you will, you fellows can stay the night here in the house; we have several spare bedrooms, and I believe the prisoners will be okay where they are. And you can put the suitcases in this tool room, I have a lock for the door; and far as I know I'm the only one with a key," Phil said, as he opened the door for Martin and me to store the suitcases.

"I sure hope so, my good man, I'll let you in on a little secret...all the money that was taken out of the Fort Worth bank is in those two suitcases."

Phil Coker didn't quite know what to say about that. He opened the back door and invited Martin and me into his kitchen. "It will be just a minute, gentlemen, I'm just finishing up. Go ahead and sit down at the table if you like," Mrs. Coker said. Phil pulled out a chair as she motioned for us to take a seat.

Maggie began by pouring a mug of steaming hot coffee for each of us. "Now the cream and sugar is already on the table, if you want to do a little doctoring."

"Black is fine with me, and I know Martin likes hizzen black. Mrs. Maggie, y'all are some fine folks, taking us in like you've done...How much do you think the operation for your son will cost? That has been on my mind."

"We're not sure, as of right now, Marshal, you know how things keep going up. Seems we've had the money several times, but have had to spend it in other ways."

"My wife is talking about our other son, Jerry, I was telling you about, earlier."

"Now. Phil, I wasn't going to bring that subject up, I know how it upsets you."

"Well, you know how he has bled us dry and we've gone in hock to the bank in Albany."

I could tell by Maggie's expression that she had had about enough of her son's trifling ways, and she changed the subject by saying, "I have made up a basket of food for one of you to carry to the men in the barn; I think it will hold them over until morning."

We also had a fine meal. The rain had stopped and we sat around and talked for a spell before going to bed. The dogs' barking woke me up several times during the night; I guess the family was used to that sort of thing, owning so many dogs. 'Course now, I wouldn't put up with that racket any longer that it takes to boil water.

Chapter Five

A Sad Story To Come

When I woke up I heard Mrs. Coker stirring around in the kitchen. The aroma of fresh coffee filtered all through the big house. I called to Martin to wake up and went ahead and dressed for the day. Maggie was finishing up breakfast and had the basket ready to carry to the prisoners. Martin volunteered for the chore and said he would swing by the outhouse on the way back, and then be in to have breakfast with us.

We waited on Martin for quite some time. We just thought he was talking to the men not realizing how much time had crept by.

"Well, let's not let breakfast get cold; I'll go ahead and turn thanks and we can start enjoying a hot breakfast." Phil Coker bowed his head to pray. I guess you might say we waited on Martin: 'like one hog waits on another at the trough'.

"Marshal, I apologize for the dogs last night; I don't know what riled their dander several times," Mr. Coker said.

"Marshal, I hate your deputy is missing out on a good, hot breakfast," Mrs. Maggie said, getting up and looking out the back door toward the barn. "You don't reckon something happened to him, do you?"

I thought, anything is possible, but Martin is very level headed. "I'm through eating...Mrs. Maggie, I don't know when I have enjoyed a meal like this in a while...I'll ease off to the barn and check on him."

"You tell 'em I won't put up the food until he comes to breakfast."

Mr. Coker said he was going to the living room to fill his pipe and then would come right on down to the barn; he had some pressing chores to do, since it had stopped raining. I moseyed on out of the kitchen onto the back porch. I to surveyed the back yard and the stables and barn in the distance. I walked down the steps and started down the well beaten path toward the barn. Then I had the surprise of my life.

"Hold it right there, Marshal! And don't you turn around or I'll cut you in two. I'm holding a fully loaded Henry."

Well, since my mama didn't raise a fool, I take everyone at their word, until I can process its veracity. The voice behind me sounded as serious as a heart attack. I froze - waiting on the next command from the voice behind me; knowing full well I didn't want to get shot in the back, or front either, for that matter.

"Take out your Colt, Marshal, real slow an' easy, and throw it behind you."

I quickly did as I was told, still not turning around to see who it was. The next voice I heard was that of Mr. Coker.

"Jerry, you drop that rifle right now! That is the marshal from Fort Worth."

"You stay out of this, Pa, and unlock the tool room door, I think my ship has done come in right here under my nose."

At times I'm not the sharpest knife in the drawer, but I can add two and two; now I know what the dogs were barking about last night. That's right; Mr. Coker's son rode in late last night and saw the lantern burning in the barn. As he was unsaddling his mount I'm sure he met and conversed with Hector Lopez, the temporary stage driver who killed 'ol Tom and Gail - the guys who stole the money in the first place. It probably didn't take him long to find out what business Jerry was trying to get into. He must have told him about the suitcases with all the money from the bank. It seems 'birds of a feather flock together'.

"If I have to beg, Jerry I will, please put that gun down; don't get in any more trouble, son."

"I'm already in trouble, Pa. I killed that deputy who brought the breakfast to the men in the barn this morning, after I found out all that bank money was in that tool room you have under lock and key. I'm going to Mexico."

"No, Jerry, I will not open the door for you, that is not your money, I beg of you don't!"

Jerry started toward his pa, still holding the rifle on me. He walked up the doorsteps. Now at this juncture I was lost for an idea. Knowing Martin was dead and I might be next, a miracle would be nice. I stood helplessly thinking: 'God does work in mysterious ways,' But, I had no faith; I was sure my time as a lawman had run out.

"I said give me that key, old man; I'm gonna be rich in a few minutes!" Jerry shouted. He struck his father with the butt of his Henry rifle, knocking him to the floor. As Jerry leaned over his father to get the key, Mrs. Coker stepped through the kitchen door, She was holding a Henry rifle, pointed right at Jerry.

"Jerry today is your birthday; twenty one years ago I brought you into this old world," as Jerry looked up at his mother his eyes grew as big as saucers, "and I believe it would be fitting for me to take you out of this world." And the rest is history. Mrs. Coker pulled the trigger, and when the Henry spoke it blew her son off the porch; he never moved again. She leaned the rifle against the wall and slowly walked back into the kitchen.

I ran up the steps to see if I could give some assistance to Mr. Coker, who was trying to get up. It seemed he was more interested in his wife's condition than that of his son sprawled out in the yard. After I managed to get Mr. Coker on his feet, and made sure his jaw wasn't broken, he invited me to come in. We found his wife sitting in the bedroom with the crippled boy, where he sat in a wheel chair.

"You gonna be all right, Maggie dear?" Phil Coker asked, placing his hand on her shoulder.

I was actually standing close enough to detect a smile come across her lips for a split second. I could tell she was trying to get the words out.

She lay her hand on John's crippled legs..."I know where this son is going when he dies." I stood for a minute letting this sink in. She looked up and caught my gaze. "Marshal, will you help Phil bury the boy lying out in our back yard. And don't you all worry. I'll have dinner ready when you two get back."

Phil Coker and I left the house and made our way on down to the barn, still not knowing what we would find; Jerry said he had killed Martin. And I was sure the three men were still chained up, since I was the one with the key to the hand-cuffs.

"I'll go and hitch up a horse for the buckboard while you check on the prisoners and your deputy," Phil Coker explained, as we neared the front of the barn.

The barn door was wide open; I walked on in, never expecting to find anything but another dead body. I quickly cast an eye over toward the three men and saw they were still chained, just as I had left them last night. I eased on over to where poor ole Martin was lying - face down - with a five-prong pitch-fork beside him. Up around his neck and shoulders was a bloody mess. As I rolled him over I noticed he wasn't wearing a gun belt...then I added two and two and realized that Jerry had stripped Martin of his gun rigging and had given it to Hector Lopez. I drew my pistol and spun around, but not in time to keep from taking a slug in my left shoulder. Thanks to Ray Green (who was cuffed and chained next to Hector Lopez) for jerking the big chain twice, causing him to miss me two more times. I got off the fatal shot; the slug caught Hector right between the eyes. He fell to the hay covered ground, and never moved again.

I took the key out of my pocket and slowly walked over to Ray Green. "Man, I owe you one, that son-of-a bitch would have filled me full of holes if you hadn't kept snatching that chain."

"Marshal, I couldn't just sit here on this bale of hay and let him kill you in cold blood."

"Well, just between you and me and that barn door over there, you have just been pardoned. Catch your mount in the pasture. Your saddle and gun rigging is in the stage. Stay out of trouble!"

"You mean I'm free to go?"

"That right, I've been thinking, you haven't broken any law."

"What about me, Marshal, I ain't did nothing bad, have I?" old Darby Black pleaded.

"What about it, Ray, will you take care of him and keep him out of trouble?"

"I guess so Marshal, his bark in worse than his bite, anyway."

"The same goes for you, Darby, but first, let me ask a favor of you two men. Since this wound in my left arm is giving me some problems...could you give me and Phil Coker a hand burying the three men? He's hitching up the buckboard now."

"Marshal, we'd be more than glad to."

By the time the wagon was hitched to the horses and the bodies were loaded, I was feeling woozy and about to faint.

"I need to get you in the house, Marshal, one of you fellows give me a hand."

When Mrs. Coker saw the two holes in my shirt and all the blood I had lost, she began to scold me for not coming to the house to get help sooner.

"Here," she said, "let me help you with that shirt; it needs to be washed anyway. And you are going to get over there where it's cool and lie down, while I bandage up that shoulder."

"But I need to help with the burying!" I protested.

"You do what I've told you or somebody will be burying you, tomorrow."

Really she was right, I did need to sit down.

"Don't you fret, Marshal, me and the two men can take care of this job."

"Here Phil...take your Bible and say a few words over the deceased." That was the last thing I actually remember, until Mrs. Coker brought me a tray with my dinner.

"Now, now, sweet lady, I could have gotten up and come to the dining table."

"Now, Marshal Blunt, me and my wife has talked it over; we think you should stay off your feet a couple of days, until that wound in your shoulder mends a smidgen. It did lot of bleeding, and you don't want to break it loose and start bleeding again."

"That's right, Marshal, besides you can't go to Fort Worth until the river goes down," Mrs. Coker said, agreeing with her husband. It didn't take to much convincing for me to go along with their advice. My shoulder was worse than I had originally thought. After the third day I was fit as a fiddle and Phil Coker brought in some good news - according how you wanted to take it.

"I just wanted you know I heard they have the ferry on Fowler River in service this morning, and the river is back in its bank," Phil reported.

"That is good news, I'm sure they need to get the stagecoach back in service, and I just imagine the Fort Worth Bank needs their money." I flexed my arm, showing them I had improved.

"One other thing Maggie and I wanted to discuss with you, Marshal, what about us and our son, John, hitching a ride with you on the stage when you leave?"

"What about the ranch and feeding of the animals while you're gone to the hospital with your son?"

Phil Coker looked at his wife, then explained. "Maggie's sister, who lives not far from here, has agreed that she and her husband will be more than glad to move in and keep the ranch up, until we get back from the hospital."

"Well, I say you can't beat that offer with a big stick, and you are more than welcome to ride along with me on the stage. And one other thing - I have a big house in Fort Worth; you are welcome to stay as long as need be."

"Would you be leaving in the morning?" Mrs. Coker asked. "If so, I will start getting ready to go."

I could see Mrs. Coker had new hope for her now only son. I prayed she didn't have her expectations up too high; it would be a sad thing if the doctor in Houston had given her false hope.

"Yes, I think that will be fine," I responded.

"I'll ride over and tell her sister and her husband to be here when we leave in the morning." Phil Coker said, as he turned to leave.

I guess I should have thanked him, if I had of thought of it in time. Whether the family knew it or not, a stage going down the road was an open target for every cutthroat in Texas. And we had quite a stretch of road and several days to travel before we would arrive in Fort Worth. Oh well, we'd have a good cook and nurse along for the ride, anyway.

The next morning the sister and her husband were knocking on the door before we had eaten breakfast. Phil was outside hooking the team to the stagecoach and Mrs. Coker was busy as a bee - cooking breakfast and running back and forth packing,. 'Course her sister, Marge, gave her a hand with things once she arrived, and the husband, Jeff, gave Phil a hand with the harness for the team. Soon we all ate a filling breakfast. Marge volunteered to do the dishes so we could be on our way. I asked Mr. Coker to carry one of the suitcases. Mrs. Coker brought up the rear, pushing John in the wheelchair. After loading John and the two suitcases, Phil and I climbed up in the driver's seat, turned the stage around, and headed toward the river crossing.

When we arrived there was no waiting at the river, and the barge was on our side. The attendant motioned us onto the barge; as he pulled the rope we began to move toward the east side of the river. I noticed a couple of the horses weren't all that fond of crossing the river. Phil quickly jumped off the stage and calmed the animals down by holding a tight rein and covering their eyes until we made it to the other side.

"What do you folks think about us staying in a hotel tonight in Albany and getting an early start in the morning? We should, with luck, make it to Fort Worth by dark."

Phil was all for the idea; so our journey began as soon as we got the stagecoach onto dry land. Now, with Flower River behind us, and a dry road between us and the town of Albany, I thought we were making good time. There was still in front of us a piece of road that was rough and rocky - a hard course to drive - even for a professional, experienced stage driver...which I was not. Phil Coker had turned the driving over to me the first two miles of our trip, said he 'barely could drive one horse, certainly not a team of four'.

Oh well, not being familiar with this piece of the road, I misjudged the curve; it was sharper than I thought. As I looked at the damaged back spoke wheel, I knew I should have slowed down, but it was 'too late to close the stable door after the horse has gotten out'. The stage had scuffed off and slid down an embankment, hitting a rock as big as the stage itself, busting the back wheel.

"What do you think, Phil?" I asked as we both looked on.

"No use crying over spilled milk, Marshal, but without a wheel it looks like this is far as we go, without a miracle."

"Well, sir, it may not be a miracle, but it looks like we got some help coming our way."

"Marshal, I hope you speak Indian language better than I do," Phil said, as he observed the feathers and other Indian garb the dozen or so men were wearing.

I guess it was the leader who rode up close to us and began saying something neither I nor Phil could understand. I began to shake my head indicating I didn't understand. I looked at Phil; he shrugged his shoulders and twisted his mouth. I knew what that meant. The Indian began licking his lips and rubbing his belly, pointing toward the stage.

"Y'all are a hunting party, and hungry." I tried to explain. He began jabbering again. "Are you sure you don't understand what he is saying?" I said, turning to Phil.

"Well, what little I know, he says he's hungry and they need something to eat."

"This ain't no rolling store, you dumb Indian, it's a stage. I got something hanging on my side that will fill your red bellies, but I don't have but six chunks of lead, and that isn't enough to go around." He began to jabber again and started pointing to the suitcases on top of the stage. I noticed that at least half of the scallywags were carrying rifles. I also knew they had counted the odds: only one pistol, and a dozen braves; why, they could have taken what they wanted from us. But to save our hair I would have tried most anything. I knew they didn't want the money. I looked behind the stage where we still had three horse tied and tagging along: my horse, Martin's and Hector Lopez's. I walked back to the horse that belonged to Hector Lopez, untied it from the stage, and eased over to the Indian sitting in front of the pack. I offered him the reins. He quickly turned around to the mob following him and held up the reins. They jabbered as they turned their painted ponies and rode away.

I could see Phil Coker breathe a sigh of relief as the thieving bunch of Indians rode out of sight. 'Course, I thought about doing a couple of cartwheels myself.

"Them Indians thought they really put one over on us, flexing their muscles into giving them a fine riding horse."

"Do you think they will be back?" Phil asked.

"Oh no, that bunch won't, but they may tell the other scavengers at camp, and since we still have two good horses, we may get some more Indians visitors tomorrow."

"What about our problem at hand, Marshal?"

"Believe it or not, I have given it some thought, and this is what I have come up with, we still got two good horses rested up, let's tie the two suitcases on Martin's horse, and I'll ride mine on into Albany and hope to get there before the bank closes. I'll put the money in their bank and have them send a telegram to Fort Worth Bank telling them they have their money. Then I will buy a wheel for the stage and hightail it back here as fast as I can."

"Now, Marshal, I was thinking along those same lines myself, except I had forgot about the money in the two suitcases."

Phil and I didn't lose any time tying the suitcases on Martin's horse. I straddled my horse and was on my way. I reckon I hadn't gone more than five or six miles when I stopped to water the horses, fill my canteen and get a swig myself, before I crossed a small stream. I don't mind telling you I pushed the horses pretty hard, but soon the town of Albany came into sight. I didn't know it at the time, but I had killed two birds with one stone. Before going to the bank I stopped by the stage depot and blacksmith shop. I explained to Big John about the stage driver and what had happened to the stage.

"Well now, since the stage belongs to the stage line, it is my place to keep it fixed. I have a buckboard hitched with two fresh horses sitting right outside. Now, since I'm not busy, I'll throw a wheel in the back and be on my way to fix the broken wheel."

I explained I was bringing a rancher and his family back to Albany to spend the night.

He suggested I save the horses, since a stagecoach wheel would be too heavy for a single horse to carry. "Do your business up the street at the bank and come back and wait for me here; then we will go up to the café and eat supper."

Chapter Six

Getting The Job Done

I straddled my horse and made a beeline for the bank while Big John threw a wheel in the buckboard and tore out to repair the stage. I caused some attention when I tied up in front of the bank with two suitcases. Then I near caused a panic when I came dragging them in the front door.

"I'm the U.S. Marshal over in Fort Worth; my name is William Blunt. I need for you to lock these two suitcases in your vault until the Fort Worth Bank can make arrangements to come and get them"

"Is Mr. Jessie Brooks still president of the bank over there in Fort Worth?"

"Well, he was when I left a week ago. I been tracking down the bank robbers, and I'm sad to say most everyone involved is dead.

"Marshal, I'm glad to help out another bank. My name is Cary Cobb; I try to be president and janitor around here."

"Now sir, as far as I know, this is how Tom Murdock and Gail Fleming packed the money they stole from the bank. The suitcases have never been opened but have made a round, still tied with the same rope on each one."

Mr. Cobb motioned for two tellers to come and get the suitcases and put them in the bank vault. "If you have time, Marshal, I would like for us to sign some papers, and we'll ask the two tellers to witness it, showing that I have the money in our bank."

There was one thing for sure, I had time to kill. Now, in my way of thinking it would be at least two or three hours before Big John would be back with the stage. So I milled around town for quite some time looking, then rode on down to the stage depot to wait on Big John to get back. There was a bench sitting out on the porch of the depot, that looked quite comfortable, which I took advantage of. I sat and watched the sun disappear and watched the town begin to close down, except for the saloons, and they began to get more lively.

I guess due to the hard day I had had, I must have dozed off; I went hard and fast asleep. To make a long story short, thank goodness for some gun happy galoot out in the middle of Main Street shooting at the moon. I quickly took out my timepiece and looked at the time; more than two hours had passed since I had been sitting here on this bench. Well, it didn't take a Philadelphia lawyer to figure that something had gone wrong...Big John should have been here by now.

I thought I'd give him a few more minutes. Meanwhile, I'd run up the street to the café to get a bite to eat and then head out to check on Big John. The café was about to close; I ordered coffee and a roast beef sandwich. While I was waiting, I overheard a conversation at a nearby table that certainly got me to thinking.

"Something has got to be done about that bunch of renegade Indians that has left the reservation," said one of the men sitting at the table nearby. "That's for sure, the troops may need to come back in and do their work," was the agreement of another at the table, "I done had my run-in with the Indians, and it could have been a lot worse."

I finished eating my sandwich, all the while hoping Big John hadn't had a visit from the renegades.

I thanked God for a clear night and a full moon overhead. I pushed my horse pretty hard thinking I would run into them coming my way any minute, but that was wishful thinking. I saw the stage up ahead, and just to play it safe, I dismounted a ways before I reached it, and led my horse, very quietly, toward it. Now, as I approached the stage, it was plain to see also the buckboard that Big John had driven. There were no horses, not even the two that were pulling the buckboard.

I tied my reins to a low hanging limb and very quietly eased up to the stage. As I crawled to the stage coach I could faintly hear a woman's voice. "It going to be alright, John...Daddy is going to be fine; he'll be back after while." It was Mrs. Coker, talking to her son.

"Mrs. Coker! It is the marshal; don't yell out, I am coming inside the stage." Mrs. Coker and the boy were sitting down in the floorboard between the front and back seat, nearly covered with a quilt. "Tell me what happened Mrs. Coker, was it Indians?" I asked, sitting down in the front seat of the stage and leaning back to whisper.

"Yes, it was, Marshal."

"Tell the marshal about the paint!" said the boy.

"That's right, Marshal, they were all painted up, I don't believe it was the same bunch you gave the horses to," Mrs. Coker explained.

"Could you tell how many of them, there were?"

"No, not really, me and John laid down in the bottom of the stage and stayed covered up. I don't think they even knew we were in the stage."

"Marshal, there were eight of them," said the boy.

"Are you sure, I'm going after them."

"Yes sir, there were only eight," the boy said, trying to raise up. "I counted them as they rode up."

"Well, tell me just exactly what happened, Mrs. Coker."

"As you know, you left Phil and myself, along with John, here at the stage to go to get a wheel for the stage coach...well, we made ourselves as comfortable as possible to wait...now we wasn't keeping up with the time, but Phil and I knew it was getting late. We soon heard a wagon coming and Phil excused himself and stepped out of the stagecoach to see who it was. It turned out to be the man bringing the wheel to fix the stage. Phil and the man quickly unloaded the wheel, and the proper tools to change the broken wheel. As I said, it was getting late, but they had finished the chore and we were ready to leave when they saw the Indians come riding up. John and I ducked down and covered up. It 'peared that the man that brought the wheel knew the Indian language - the way they kept shouting at each other."

"That was Big John, the blacksmith and manager of the stage line in Albany."

Well he wasn't going to let them take the horses; I could tell he put up a fight."

"That right, Marshal, I was peeping when Pa tried to help Big John, as you call him. Yes sir, he was about to get the best of 'em and one Indian picked up a rock and struck Big John in the head."

"Do you think it killed him?"

"No sir, it knocked him out long enough for the Indians to tie him up and put him on a horse."

"What about your pa?" I asked the boy.

"They just manhandled Pa, and they also put him put on a horse and rode off."

"Could you tell if any of them had guns?"

"Yes sir, I know at least three of them had rifles," answered the boy. "And I can tell you something else, Marshal, they didn't go far; it was getting dark and Indians don't fight or travel at night. They are camped in that valley way down there," he said pointing downhill. "I could see their camp fire when they first stopped."

"You are very observant, John, you'd make a good detective," I said getting out of the stage.

"You think so, Marshal?" John quickly asked.

"Now, now, we'll have no more talk like that, Marshal... after seeing you nearly get killed. I don't need no law men in the family."

I went ahead and got out of the stage and shut the door. "I am going to ride on down to that valley, and see about getting Phil and Big John back from the renegades before morning."

As I started to walk off I thought I heard Mrs. Coker say something to me, so I turned back around. She was trying to hand me two gun belts through the stagecoach window. "You may need these, Marshal, there are eight Indians and you have only got six slugs in your Colt."

I remembered, now, throwing Martin's and Hector Lopez's gun rigging in the stage with the saddles. "I thank you very much, Mrs. Coker, I certainly will if I get into a gun battle with that bunch of heathens." I went ahead and buckled Martin's gun belt around me and hung the other gun rigging around my neck; at least I had enough fire power.

I rode as close as I could to the camp, without possibly waking the bunch of buzzards. I then watched my steps so not to break a twig underfoot, as I eased closer. As I said earlier, the full moon was a big help. As I expected there was Phil and Big John, tied to a stake, just inside their camp. At least they weren't dead; I took my spyglass and checked them out, to make sure I saw both of then moving.

I squatted down behind some thick bushes to come up with a plan, so I wouldn't get shot again. My shoulder was just now getting well from the other shooting. If Elizabeth, my wife, knew that I had gotten shot, and a fixing to get in a shoot scrap with these bunch of Indians, she would leave me for sure. Knowing her, she would go back east. The one thing I needed to be sure about, what was I going to do when it got daylight? One idea stuck me that didn't sound half way bad, I'd just sneak around through the camp and cut their mangy throats while they were asleep; but I didn't have a knife; big deal, I thought, just tiptoe over to the closest Indian, knock him in the head with my pistol, and get his knife. Yeah, I thought, he'd probably bellow like a wounded buffalo, and wake the whole thieving bunch up.

No, I'd wait until morning and ride through the camp shooting everything that walked, crept, or crawled, and if I didn't get everything the first pass, I'd come back through the second time shooting. I thought for a minute, 'no, I will probably get shot at, and the dumb Indian shooting at my body will miss and accidentally hit me in the head, and that ain't good. Maybe if I could get to Phil Coker and Big John, and manage to cut them loose, they could help. But if I gave them one of my Colts, that would leave me with only six shots between eight Indians. Since neither Big John nor Phil Coker wear pistols what makes me think they could hit a barn with a gun in the first place'? I put that idea to rest and decided to just play it by ear.

As the moon went down, and before the sun started coming up, it turned really dark and chilly. As far as I could tell, I was standing about mid-ways of the outer edge of the camp. I didn't need to look at my pocket watch; one could just tell dawn was coming; the birds and other wild life, including bugs and flies, began to greet the new day dawning.

I began to flex my gun hand and made sure all three pistols were fully loaded. I could almost hear the dawn breaking. It began to get lighter and lighter, as the sun began filtering through the branches behind me. I could see clearly now, as my eyes adjusted to the light, but I could only count six Indians lying around. I spied the team horses - and probably the pair of horses that was pulling the buckboard; they were tied up separately from the Indian ponies.

The Indian lying no more than twenty feet right in front of me began to roll around. I noticed a rifle lying very close to him. I could see more clearly now, and saw that the Indian lying beside him also had a rifle. Well, I could at least take two guns out of the equation, since the boy said he had only seen three rifles among the renegades.

As I stood there waiting for something or someone to make the first move, much began to run through my mind; such as what the Bible says: 'Thou shall not kill, don't spill innocent blood...' and the scriptures went on. I heard a noise and turned my head toward Phil and Big John, I couldn't tell what they were saying, but could see they were trying to get loose. Then, here came an Indian walking out of the woods, I hadn't counted...that made seven, and he appeared to be walking straight for Phil and Big John. I will never know if he was going to cut them loose, or cut their throats.

As he drew closer he walked right in front of me. I already had my pistol out, and shot him right through the heart. It seemed by being close range, the noise of the shot was muffled. All I know is - the two Indians lying right in front of me jumped up with their rifles and began to look all around; I fired two more shots; they buckled at the knees and bit the dust.

Three from eight leaves five. I'll be the first to admit I don't know the mind of Indians but here came the eighth Indian running out of the woods toward Phil and Big John. Well, needless to say, I folded him up like a cheap accordion. I'm no mathematician, but that still left four more Indians. In the heat of things it seemed to me that the two men tied to the stakes were the problem and were causing all the noise. I was pretty much hidden in the bushes and don't think I was even noticed. Here came two more Indians, right for Phil and Big John, one had a rifle and the other had a big knife. It was like shooting fish in a barrel, my Colt was smoking hot...and empty... When I holstered it and drew Martin's pistol to finish the job, I saw the last of the thieving buzzards in the circle of the camp. They were disoriented and didn't know where to run or fight; it was a long shot for a hand gun, but I made up their minds for them.

I stood still for a minute, it was as quiet as a Wednesday night prayer service, even the birds and crickets silenced their songs. I slowly walked over to the dead Indian closest to Phil and Big John, relieved him of his knife, and began to cut the ropes to free the men. Usually, you don't hear grown men cry, or pray in public, in Texas, but we had to thank God for a miracle, as we knelt on the ground, looking up into a clear blue sky.

As the three of us rose to our feet, we surveyed the overnight camp and the eight corpses lying all around.

"What about the Indians?" Phil Coker asked.

"Oh yeah, the Indians..." I said, "gather up all the rifles they have and take them with us."

"I meant about the dead Indians," Phil said, reaching down to pick up a rifle.

"Not to give you a short answer, my good man, but they are all dead," explained Big John, "and the Indians don't bury their dead, so why should we... is that what you meant?"

"Oh, well, it just doesn't seem right, does it?"

"It's their religion, and who are we to interfere, but we do need to take the bridles off their horses, and let them go free. I wouldn't think they go along with the Indian foolishness."

As we approached the stagecoach with the four horse team and the two buckboard horses, Mrs. Coker and John had their own prayer meeting, seeing we were all safe. The lot of us didn't lose any time hitching up and getting the show on the road. We knew I had exterminated one bunch of renegades; but were there others that had left the reservation, doing mischief? After arriving in Albany, Big John found our there was a young, married couple wanting fare to Houston; he knew the Cokers were headed to Houston, also. He exchanged teams and sent the stage eastward, with instructions to stop only at the stage relay stations.

I spent the night in the hotel and decided to get an early start the next morning. My plans were to take both horses, mine and Martin's, and exchange horses every few miles to rest them up. I hoped to arrive in Fort Worth by early evening.

Since I had to pass my hardware store and gun repair shop before I reached home, I decided to stop and catch up on the news...I hadn't been here in over a week. My son was there keeping the store, and all he had was bad news; the first thing out of his mouth was... "George Simmons has been shot". George was my other deputy, and I hated to tell him that Martin Travick had also been killed.

"Well, what happened Billy?"

"First of all, Father, Butch Parlay was the one that shot George...naturally he was drunk, and said he shot Deputy George in self defense."

"Was it self defense?" I asked.

"According to the whole town...half says it was, an and the other half says it wasn't"

"What do you say, did you see the shooting?"

"Yes sir, but I'm not the law, or the judge."

"Billy, just back up and tell me what happened."

"Me and George Simmons was here in the hardware store, standing right over there." He pointed and went on with his story, "With nothing else to do, George was making his rounds and wandered off in here to see if me or mother had heard from you, since you had been gone. He and I had heard some shooting up the street, out in front of the Silver Dollar Saloon. We just figured it was a cowboy letting off a little steam, and went on talking. I told him we hadn't heard a word, and I guess you'd be back when we saw you coming. About the time George decided to finish his round, Butch Parlay staggered in, I mean literally staggered in, drunk as a pole cat. 'I want to buy some bullets,' he said with a slurry, thick tongue, slinging his pistol all around. 'You don't need anymore bullets, Butch, why don't you go on home and sleep it off before you hurt yourself or somebody.' George told him, as nice as he could. Butch went to cursing and carrying on like you never heard, 'who do you think you are? You ain't my boss,' he said. We didn't know whether he had another bullet in his pistol or not."

"What happened then?" I asked,

"I could tell that Deputy George was getting fed up with his vulgar mouth. He drew his pistol. I said, 'Holster your pistol and get out of this store before I haul you to jail'. Well, Butch did as he was told and staggered on outside. Personally, I thought it was all over, and walked with George to the door. It was getting late and I was fixing to close anyway. When he and I stepped out on the boardwalk in front of the hardware store there stood Butch, not more than ten feet away, facing us with his pistol pointed right at Deputy George. He said, 'You done drawn down on me, boy, now it's my turn,' and he pulled the trigger, shooting Deputy George right through the heart."

"And you saw the whole thing?"

"That's right, Father, there were some folks standing across the street from us who said they saw the whole thing, too."

"Did George go for his pistol after he saw Butch Parlay was standing there with his pistol trained on him," I asked.

"Yes sir, George did reach for his pistol, and he had it in his hand when he fell to the porch. It wasn't but a second, it seems like, that folks started gathering around...and every time somebody would walk up, 'It was self defense,' Butch would say... 'he pulled his pistol on me first.' You can see, Father, most townsfolk didn't know what to believe."

"But you are saying: that Butch Parlay shot George, my deputy, down in cold-blood?"

"That's right, Father, it wasn't a fair fight, and Deputy George was just doing his job. And I might add, you will find out anyway, Butch Parlay's old man has been up town shooting off his mouth about what he was going to do to anybody that comes to their spread, snooping around asking questions."

"Well, I can tell him one thing, I am the law and I got the right to go out there on his ranch anytime I want to, and ask as many questions as I need to. If he causes trouble, it's all up to him. People are breaking the law when they are not abiding by the law. Ignorance is no excuse, in sight of the law, no matter who it might be."

Chapter Seven

The Parlay Case Grew Worse

"Oh well, let me get on home and see your mother, I'll see you at supper." And with those few words and a tired body from riding all day, I left the hardware store and headed home.

"Well it's about time you get home where you belong, William Blunt," Elizabeth scolded, as I walked into the kitchen where she was cooking supper.

"Just doing my job, my dear," I said, walking over putting my arms around her.

I could hear her when she sniffed a time or two. "For Pete's sake William, have you taken a bath since you've been gone?" She took a step back and looked me up and down, "Just look at you, dear, you are a disgrace; you look like a bear."

"At least I got all the money back that was robbed from the bank." I couldn't help but notice Elizabeth adjusting her specks back and forth on her nose.

"William, is that a hole in the new shirt I bought you for your birthday?"

"I'm afraid so, Darling, and there is a hole in the back also, where the slug came out."

Elizabeth turned white as a sheet and began to buckle at the knees. "Help me sit down William, I feel faint." I soon had her subdued, and Billy made it home from the hardware store.

"I guess you are going to tell your father about all the excitement the town had the first part of the week?" Elizabeth directed her question across the table to Billy, our son. Billy quickly looked at me.

"I stopped by the hardware store before I came home, and he enlightened me on how George was murdered by Butch Parlay."

Elizabeth twisted her mouth. "And I guess you'll be running off again," Elizabeth said, dabbing the corner of her mouth with her napkin.

"Well, that all depends."

"I just prefer we don't discuss it in the confines of our home." And that was that, I had no idea when Elizabeth would come to grips with the fact she was married to a lawman, like it or not. It's hard to have your wife oppose everything you do. If one knew the truth...Elizabeth would just as soon sweep this innocence of George's murder under the rug. I had a job to do, and I would not shove it on the back burner, I would uphold the law as long as I wore the badge.

I did get me a hot bath and shave before I went to bed; it was the only way Elizabeth would let me sleep in the same bed with her. She said she was so ashamed of me, the way I looked, and so glad our pastor didn't come by before I cleaned myself up. I thought 'if our pastor knew what I'd been through this past week he would have prayed for me every five minutes. For crying out loud, I'm lucky to be alive.' What is it they say: 'there is no place like home', and that's a fact; I'd done gotten use to my goose down feather bed.

'Early to bed and early to rise, makes one healthy, wealthy and wise', my father was always quoting to me when I was a lad coming up back east. I presume it works equally as well out West. I've always been an early riser and this day was no exception, I had lots of work to be catching up on, so I rolled out of bed without even awaking Elizabeth. Dawn was just beginning to break when I eased off down to the stable and saddled my horse for the day. I had intentions of riding over to Randy Parlay's spread later on, to talk to him about his boy, Butch Parlay. And then I was warned I might be taking my own life in my hands; but what kind of fool would just come running out of the house and start shooting, when I came riding up to his spread, without any reason.

Mr. Tillman was opening up his feed and seed store when I came riding by. "Morning to you, Marshal, good to see you back in town, and sorry about all your deputies getting killed." Bad news travels fast out west, I thought.

"It's sure good to have the money back in the bank," I said, dismounting in front of his store, "tell me something, Tillman,, what do you know about my deputy getting shot by Butch Parlay?"

"Actually, no more than what I've heard around town, and what your boy has told me."

I had a little time to kill before I opened the hardware store, so I eased over to where Tillman stood, sweeping the porch in front of his place of business.

"Do you think Butch shot my deputy in self-defense?"

"Now, Marshal, I don't really know...but I wouldn't believe Butch Parlay if he was standing on a stack of Bibles, and that goes for the whole family. They owe me money right now...I'll probably never get."

"You're on the town council do you think I ought to bring him in for questioning?"

Tillman stop sweeping and propped up on his broom. "Marshal, I'm glad I'm not in your boots this morning...but, yes...anytime there is a killing there should be a hearing by a judge, to get the straight of things one way or the other."

"What about the other city council members?" I asked.

"We've done met and talked while you were gone out of town, and they believe the same way I do, we just hate that it's you that has to do the job. You know how that whole bunch of Parlays are, they'd just soon shoot you as look at you; sad to say but it's the gospel truth."

"There isn't much encouragement this morning. As soon as Billy gets here to watch the hardware store I was planning to ride out to Old Man Parlay's spread, and talk to him about his boy coming into town for questioning."

"Well, I'm damn sure I wouldn't ride out there alone...excuse my French."

"Are you saying I should round up a posse and go out there?" I asked.

"I'm saying...I wouldn't go out to Old Man Parlay's ranch alone this morning," Mr. Tillman repeated, then resumed sweeping.

"I'll give it some thought." I turned and started back to the hitching post where my horse was standing. I didn't mount up but led my horse on over to my store giving Mr. Tillman's advice lots of consideration. This job had gotten me shot one time, and nearly shot a dozen times since. But I made up this bed...so I would have to sleep in it.

I opened up shop, propped the doors open, and waited for Billy to come; but I could never get Old Man Parlay off my mind. Was I losing my grip, or getting too old for this job? One thing for sure, I was going out there this morning right by myself; I was the U.S. Marshal and it was my job. I would be on official law business, and if he wanted to make it bad for himself then he would suffer the consequences.

The first thing Billy asked me when he came in was, "Are you going out to see Old Man Parlay this morning, Father?" I could tell my son was concerned about my health and safety. "Mother said you got shot in the shoulder while you were gone last week chasing the bank robbers."

"Your mother was right, Billy, and I dang near got killed two or three times." Billy didn't quite know what to say when I told him about walking into a Indian camp just at daybreak, and killing eight renegades in one shooting.

"Father, can I ride with you out to the Parlay ranch today after Mother comes in to work?" Now I didn't know what to say. "After all, I didn't get to see you all week." I don't mind telling you that did make me feel bad, not spending more time with my son.

"Let's see what your mother thinks about the idea." I went into the gun repair shop and made sure my gun belt was full of cartridges. Billy followed me into the gun shop and began to ask me questions. "Father, do you mind if I wear my gun rigging this morning while I'm with you?"

"You'd better not let your Mother hear you say that, Bill, she'll have that calf you keep talking about." We were both still laughing when Elizabeth walked into the hardware store.

"Now, what is so funny? 'Course I should know it don't take much for you two to get tickled over."

"Father wanted me to ask you if you would mind if I rode around with him today while he is on a few calls. You know I haven't seen him for over a week."

"Well, I don't mind if he doesn't, it will probably be a slow day anyway."

I saw Billy light up like new snow on the pump handle. "Let me run home and saddle my horse, Father!" Billy tore through the gun repair shop and out the back door, stopping long enough to get his gun rigging out from under the counter.

"I'll come by the stable when I get ready to go, Billy!" I yelled. I eased back in the main store where Elizabeth was sitting at the desk working on our books.

"Elizabeth, darling, I just noticed you and I have a grown son! Or have you really looked at him lately?"

"I'm afraid so, William, and he wants to be just like you; and there isn't anything I can do about it. I'm getting concerned that Billy knows more about Samuel Colt and Wild Bill Hickok than he knows about Matthew, Mark, Luke and John."

"Give him time, Darling. Is being married to a lawman all that bad?"

Elizabeth laid her pen down and turned around at the desk to face me. A smile came across her lips. "Don't make me answer that question...you have a good time with your son today."

When I came riding up to the stable Billy was sitting astride his mount with a .45 Colt tied to his leg, like a professional. I blinked my eyes and my little boy had become a man overnight. I took out my handkerchief and began to wipe my eyes.

"What's the matter, Father?" Billy asked, riding over close to me.

"That darn cotton-wood pollen burns my eyes this time of year."

As Billy and I rode along, I guess we talked about a little of everything, including Tom Murdock and his cousin Gail Fleming being killed on the stage, by the stage driver that had been hired that same day. I told Billy he was the man that had shot me in the shoulder. I also told him how I'd met the Cokers while gallivanting last week; and how Mrs. Coker shot her own son while he was holding a pistol on me.

"That's the Parlay spread up there, isn't it, Father? I've never been out here."

"Yes it is," I answered.

"Have you given it any consideration what will happen if he starts trouble for us?" I knew then that Billy had been versed in just how bad this bunch of scum was.

"You know he has four more boys, not counting Butch." Billy stated, staying right even with me.

"You want to go back? Now is the time" I said, stopping my horse in sight of the Parlay ranch house.

"Only if you turn back, Father."

"Are you scared, Billy, that shooting may start?"

"Not really, Father, but if it does do you want me to shoot to kill?" Now that question came from my own flesh and blood; was I to tell my own son to kill a living soul? What kind of father was I?

"For God's sake, Billy, what are we doing sitting here? I can't answer that question...you ask a hard thing!"

"I know, Father, but if it is right for you, isn't it alright for me?"

"Billy, Billy, Billy...if you accidentally caught a chunk of lead and died, I would never forgive myself. And I could never face your mother again.!"

"Look, Father, I been doing lots of reading here lately that says you should never think about getting shot, or putting a curse on yourself going into battle."

I then remembered I still had the star in my vest pocket that I had taken off Martin's shirt, there in the barn at the Coker's ranch. I rode over close to Billy. "Lean over this way, boy, raise your right hand and repeat after me, as I pin this deputy star on your shirt. "I promise to perform and obey the law of Fort Worth County, so help me God." I couldn't believe I had just made a deputy out of a sixteen-year-old boy. As I look back now, I did more than hang a star on Billy's shirt; I put my seal of approval on him, saying, 'I'm proud of you, my son'.

"You ready, Billy?" I asked.

A smile came across his face as wide as Texas. "As ready as I will ever be." As he and I rode up to the ranch house the dogs went to barking. We just sat on our mounts surveying the surroundings. In less than a minute Mr. Parlay walked out on the front porch toting a rifle.

"You won't need the rifle, Mr. Parlay; it's me and my deputy."

"I'll do the deciding what I need, Marshal. What are you doing trespassing on my property?" I didn't like the sound of his voice and I noticed someone standing behind the screen door.

"Just wanted to ask you some questions concerning your boy Butch; is he here today?"

"Marshal, there is nothing to discuss about my boy...besides he's not here right now."

"Oh, well, you can give Butch a message when you see him. Tell him that anytime there is a shooting and someone gets killed...there will be a hearing...performed by the judge, to see if needs to go to court or not."

"Marshal, it is an open and shut case, it was self defense."

"That what I hear Mr. Parlay, but according to the law Butch will still need to come before the judge; if it's self defense, he walks free, if it's not, there will be a court case."

"Now, Marshal, I'll be frank with you, Butch is not coming in to be railroaded and put in jail."

"Mr. Parlay, let me be frank with you, until Butch settles this matter he is wanted by the law for questioning. As a U. S. Marshal, it is my place to bring him in. You can tell him to make it easy on himself. Are you ready to ride, Billy?" He nodded and we rode off, keeping an eye on our back side. As he and I rode out of the sight of the house, Billy kept looking back.

"You see something?" I asked.

"Yes, Father, that was Butch's horse in the corral by the barn, or did you notice?"

"I'm afraid I don't know one horse from the other. What makes you sure?"

"It was a Flaxen chestnut; and his horse has a light, flaxen cream to off-color white colored mane and tail. Did you notice the horse's legs and the tips of his ears were the same color as the body?"

"I can tell right now you know more about horses than I do. And you think that Butch Parlay was there in the house?"

"Father, I just came along for the ride, you are the Marshal. And Mother told me not to bet, but if I were a betting man I would say that Butch Parlay was hunkered down in the house, peeping out the front window watching us, with a cocked Henry."

"Son, that's a pretty good analysis, I didn't say anything but I just figured Butch Parlay and his brothers were in the house waiting for us to make a move."

"Father, this has been the best day of my life - riding with you and helping out."

"Billy... I never knew you felt like this before."

"I know, Father, Mother wants me to be a lawyer or a doctor or maybe a professor. Father... I don't want that for my life, do you blame me?"

"Son, you are driving some hard questions, you know how your mother is against guns and lawmen." Billy started laughing.

"What seems to be so funny? I asked, as he and I headed back into town.

"She married you, didn't she?" I thought about what Billy said and I started laughing.

"What do you think about you and me swinging by the restaurant and getting us a piece of pie and coffee?"

"I would love to, Father."

He and I tied up at the hitching rail and started in. I couldn't help but notice my son; he was walking tall, making sure his star was polished, and his Colt was hanging low and tied to his leg, just right. Actually, Billy was wide at the shoulders and tall and slim - a good looking cowboy. He creased his wide-brim cowboy hat, and we went in and walked over to a table.

The waitress was very young and beautiful lady. She gave Billy the eye as she took our order. As we were eating our pie and sipping our coffee the subject came up again about Butch Parlay.

"Father, have you got a plan to get Butch Parlay without a fight?"

I took a big swig of my black coffee and wiped my mouth on my sleeve. "Not really, you got an idea?" I couldn't believe I was asking my sixteen-year old son for his advice.

"As you know, Father, I do a lots of reading which mother sneers at. I keep my lawman books hidden from her. But, according to the advice Bat Masterson and Doc Holiday give in their books, we can catch him with his own mistakes."

"And you know his mistakes, do you?" I asked.

"Yes, I do, Father, it's girls and whiskey. The grapevine around town says he is seeing Judy Parker - she works up at the Silver Slipper Saloon. And he meets her every night before work."

I listened, as my son had it all planned out. "You suggest we be waiting on him when he shows up, and arrest him?"

"That's about the size of it, Father, and put him in jail."

"Billy, you know when your mother gets wind of this she is going to be mad."

"I know, I know, Father, but this is what I want to do... I want to be a lawman just like you... is that so hard for Mother to understand?"

"All I know, Billy, is you and I have got to wear kid gloves with this situation. Elizabeth is very sensitive about these things."

"Will there be anything else I can get for y'all?" I quickly turned around to see our waitress standing there.

"Will you be our new deputy in town, Mr. Billy?" she asked. He caught my gaze and I just sat there, not saying a word.

"You might say I'm on a trial basis, Miss Dorothy."

"Well, I sure hope you get the job, I'll probably be seeing more of you."

As Billy looked back at me, my facial expressions were saying: 'Son, that all comes with the star you're wearing'. As Dorothy cleaned the table, she stood very close to Billy, letting her hips brush up against him several times.

In the sweetest voice I ever heard she said, "Thank you for the tip, Mr. Billy."

"Billy, if you will, take the horses on over to the stable an' unsaddle them. I'll walk over to the hardware store and close up, and mosey on to the house with your mother."

"What about Butch Parlay?"

"I haven't forgotten about him. We'll go ahead and eat supper and come back tonight."

"Can I come back with you, Father?"

I hesitated for a thought. "Oh...I guess so." It was hard to say no to Billy. I was away from home so much and he needed a father that he could look up to. I didn't think his mother went along with every thing I let him do, but I could tell this was Billy's life - following in my footsteps, wanting to be a lawman. You might say he was standing in the shadow of me, in many ways. And that made me proud in many ways. I know it goes against the grain, but in some ways Billy was right; it would be his life to live when his mother and I were dead and gone.

Chapter Eight

Catching Butch Parlay

I wondered why Elizabeth was in such a hurry fixing supper tonight, 'course now she calls it dinner. We were well into our meal when she caught Billy's gaze. "Son, I want you, after supper, to hitch up the surrey and drive me over to the school house; we're having our annual Flower Club meeting tonight." Well, I don't mind telling you, it was like she had poured cold water on Billy.

He quickly looked over at me and I smiled. "Would you two mind running me by the jail on your way to the school house, and then picking me up on the way back from the flower meeting...how long do you think it will last, Elizabeth?"

"Oh my, probably the better part of two hours, 'course we should adjourn a little before nine o'clock." The smile came back to Billy's face; I could tell he had put two and two together and realized he and I had at least two hours to put bad boy Butch's butt behind bars tonight.

While Elizabeth was getting ready to go, Billy and I eased off down to the stable. "Father, this is working out better than I thought," Billy said.

"I really don't need anything at the jail, but it gets me out of the house without your mother getting suspicious. Here is the plan: you and Elizabeth let me off at the jail and then go on over to the school. Instead of parking the surrey and waiting for your mother to get out of the meeting, 'course first make sure she is safely inside, you can then come on back and pick me up... I'll be waiting." I noticed Billy had pinned his star back on his vest and was wearing his pistol, when he came back to pick me up at the jail.

It was a rather dark night here in Fort Worth and a slight breeze was blowing out of the south. As always, there were a dozen or so gas lights hanging along Main Street in town to light the way, especially around the bank and the saloons.

"This is perfect, Billy, let's ride on down to the Silver Slipper and see if we can spot Butch's horse." The crowd had begun to gather up, like hungry cows at a feed trough. We didn't see Butch's horse. After looking with a keen eye, we rode on past the saloon. "Do you think he will come, Billy?" I asked.

"Oh yes, its past time for him, his girlfriend starts to work at seven o'clock."

"I was just thinking, with him in all this trouble, he may be here, and has his horse hidden."

"We can check around back, that is probably where he is talking to his girlfriend."

Billy and I tied up the horse and started around the saloon. Sure enough, there was Butch's horse and there was Butch, standing on the back porch of the saloon, all loved up in the arms of his girlfriend. Strangely enough, he didn't even notice us when we walked up; since there was an outhouse out back, it was commonplace for men to be coming and going. It was like taking candy from a baby. I relieved him of his pistol before he knew what happened, and shoved the girl to one side.

"You are under arrest, Butch, for shooting my deputy; make it light on yourself, you can walk or be drug."

"You ain't got nothing on me... it was self defense... George pulled a pistol on me first."

"Save your breath, Butch, you can tell it to a judge next week. Now, do you want to ride down to the jail in style or do you want me to drag you behind your horse?" Butch started down the steps toward his horse, while his girlfriend ran back inside.

"Bill, run get the surrey and bring it around back, and Butch, stop and stand right where you are."

"You wait until my pa hears about this Marshal, there is gonna be big trouble for you."

"It's up to your pa, Butch, if he wants to make trouble for himself that's fine with me. Now, get in the surrey and Billy will haul your rear down to the jail, and I will bring your horse." Well, in less time than it would take to tell it, Butch Parlay was behind bars, and Billy was on his way back to the schoolhouse to wait for his mother. I sat down at my desk, with only a dimly lit lantern, to wait for the Flower Club to adjourn. and the wife and Billy to come by and pick me up.

"Marshal, I would hate to be in your boots when the sun comes up in the morning!" Butch yelled from a cell in back of the jail. "Did you hear what I said, Marshal? You better let me go if you know what's good for you!" As I sat there listening to Butch bellow and bitch from the back room, I didn't say a word, but thought 'this I don't need, but somebody has certainly got to do the job'. I sat there thinking how Elizabeth had said she wanted Billy to be a doctor, lawyer, or anything but a lawman. I wondered now if it was too late for him to change his mind.

My thoughts continued: 'What did I have to look forward to tomorrow? Butch was right; his pa will show up in the morning with his four brothers wanting me to let Butch out of jail. They know, as well as I do, I can't do that, according to the law'. As I slid my arm back I bumped some loose change lying on the desk, and a coin fell to the floor and began to spin around and around. I watched as it soon stopped and toppled over. Was it heads or tails? It was for sure it had to be one or the other. I leaned over and picked up the coin and brought it closer to the lamp; it was heads, or it could have just as well been tails. I put the coin with the others and slid the change to the back of the rolltop desk.

With nothing more to do, and some time to kill, I opened up a book of Psalms and Proverbs that had been lying on the desk since the day I took office as U.S. Marshal. I turned so the light would come over my shoulder and opened the dust-covered, little book. I focused my eyes and noticed a verse of scripture in Proverbs that had been circled. I began to read: "There is a way which seemeth right unto a man, but the end thereof are the ways of death." I began to chew on that verse of scripture, trying to determine just what it meant. Maybe an example would be better, let's take old man Parlay...in his mind he thinks his son, Butch, shot my deputy in self defense, and is innocent. On the other hand, my son says he shot him in cold blood, without giving George a chance. Now, in my opinion, I wasn't there, but I don't think for one minute George would have harmed Butch Parlay.

I guess Butch got tired of running his mouth; he laid down on the bunk in the cell and dozed off. I heard Billy wooing the horse outside, and thought it was time to go. I locked up the jail and had started toward the surrey, when I heard shooting up at the Silver Slipper.

"Now, Elizabeth, darling, I know you are anxious to get home and tell us all the news, but would you and Billy run me up to the Silver Slipper and let me see what all the ruckus is about? I won't be long, I promise."

I never did know if Elizabeth answered yes or know...she just grunted, and Billy turned the horse around and headed for the saloon. Just as I started into the saloon, some cowboy came running out and nearly flattened me out. He straddled a horse and rode off like a swarm of bees was after him.

As the bat wings swung open, and I stepped inside, the stench of gunpowder and blood was prevalent. A dozen or more men were standing around two, dead bodies, lying in the middle of the saloon floor. Old Jake Nims was standing near the two dead cowboys.

"What happened, Jake?"

"Well, I don't rightly know, Marshal. The three came in together, I guess a hour ago, and were standing there at the bar, drinking and carrying on. And the one fellow, that just hightailed it out of here, pulled his pistol and shot the other two. Miller, standing over there, was talking to one of them earlier; he might know more than I do."

I eased over to the bar where Miller Davis was bumping his gums. "How you doing, old man?" I asked, just being sociable.

"Well, now, if it ain't the Marshal. Can I buy you a drink?"

"No Miller, Elizabeth and Billy are waiting on me out in the surrey. Jake said you were talking to one of the dead cowboys before he was shot."

"Yeah, I was, he said they had a herd of beeves bedded down just south of town, and was planning on bringing them on through tomorrow."

"Did you find out why the cowboy did the shooting?" I asked.

"No I didn't, Marshal, but the bartender thinks it was over a money issue."

"Well, money can certainly cause problems. And, by the way, since you have retired, would you be interested in a part-time deputy's job?" I thought he was going to choke on his shot of whiskey.

"Marshal, you ain't serious?!"

"Just as serious as a heart attack, I need some help down at the jail."

"Now, just what in tar-nation would I do down at the jail? I don't even own a gun...and I couldn't hit the side of the barn if I had one...and besides you've had two deputies killed in the last week."

I could see I might be barking up the wrong tree. "For Pete's sake, Miller, I'm not wanting you to shoot anyone, I just need a man to open up each morning and close up each night, and to make sure the prisoners get three square meals from the café everyday. Is that asking too much?"

"Does it pay pretty good?" Miller asked, scratching his head.

"Well, it pays more than you are making right now; you get meals and board, and I'll see that the City Council raises the pay each month."

A smile came across Miller's face. I had heard he was living with his rich sister, and she had ordered him out of the house. "You say there is a place in the jail where I can stay?"

"Oh yes there is a small bedroom with a nice comfortable bed in the back of the jail. It even has a pitcher pump and a new wood stove."

Old Miller Davis downed another shot and wiped his mouth on the back of his hand... "When do I start?"

"Right now! Is that too soon?"

"You mean I can stay at the jail tonight?" I guess I had heard right; his rich sister had run him off.

"You stay right here, Miller, my wife and son are waiting out front in our surrey. I need to get her home, and I'll be right back to open up the jail for you."

Needless to say, Elizabeth's patience was wearing thin - sitting out in front of a saloon, for God and the world to see. When Elizabeth doesn't say anything...she is really saying more that I want to hear; her silence says it all.

"Sorry to keep y'all waiting, but I managed to get it all cleared up. I'm sure you are ready to go home." I did my best to explain to Elizabeth that I was going to let them off at the house, then run back to carry Miller Davis to the jail, to spend the night and watch over the prisoner.

"I didn't know you had a prisoner in jail, William," Elizabeth commented, as I helped her out of the surrey.

"I'll explain it all when I get back." I helped Elizabeth to the front door, lit some lamps and got her settled.

"Do you mind if Billy goes with me and does the driving? I'll be right back."

She turned around and gave me a far-a-way look. "I know how 'you will be right' back turns out," she said drily. "I don't mind, after all he is sixteen years old." I turned and started for the door. "I'll be waiting up for you ,William, when you get back." How long had it been since I had heard words like that from Elizabeth? I wasn't going to let sweet words like that go to waste. I turned and walked back to her, put my arms around her waist, and pulled her to me.

I couldn't believe it, she quickly put her arms around my neck, and let her body come very close. "I thought maybe you and I could celebrate tonight."

"What brings this on, darling?" Elizabeth was like a new person. "I was elected President of the Fort Worth Flower Club tonight."

"That is great, darling, and I know you will be the best president the ladies have ever had."

"Oh... I hope so darling, the women really love me now. They also love you, William. They were all talking about the courageous thing you did last week, getting shot and all... just to get the town's money back in the bank. I'm so proud of you."

"Wonderful! But let me run; I will be right back."

Miller Davis was still standing at the bar where I had left him, of course he had long run out of money and was begging drinks. I could tell the bartender was all but having him thrown out of the place, for making a nuisance of himself: Craig Watson the funeral director had been notified, and with some help, the bodies were removed.

"Marshal, could you buy me one drink before we go?"

"No! You've had enough for one night. Where's your hat?"

"It's over there on the table where I was sitting." He started over toward the table, staggering and stumbling over everybody on his way. I was waiting and watched old Miller as he brushed by a young cowboy, sitting at a table with others playing cards. He spun around, kicking Miller in the calf of his leg, tearing his pants and leaving a nasty cut. Miller fell to the floor. holding his leg. As I walked over to Miller, I could see blood dripping from the cowboy's sharp spur, and out of Millers leg.

"Cowboy, that was uncalled for, don't you think?"

"Aw, Marshal, Ralph was just having a little fun, he didn't mean to hurt the old man," one of the men sitting at the table blurted out.

"That's right, Marshal, he didn't mean any harm;" another suggested.

I reached down and helped Miller to his feet as he strained to get up, "Go get your hat." He took a few steps and reached for his well-soiled wide-brim hat, and returned to the table where, I was still standing. The foursome was spellbound, wondering I was going to do.

"Miller, scoop up the pot in the middle of the table; now you can buy yourself a new pair of pants, and pay the sawbones to put a few stitches in your leg." Judging from my quick look and estimation - there must have been forty-five or fifty dollars piled up.

The young man who had kicked Miller quickly jumped up and got in my face. "Now you wait one damn minute, Marshal!" Without even thinking, I whipped my Colt from my holster and walloped him across the side of his head, hard enough to knock the taste out of his mouth. He spun around and hit the floor like a sack of spuds, and never moved.

"Now, Marshal, was that necessary?"

I stood for a minute looking at the group, "You tell him when he wakes up I was just having a little fun."

Billy was patiently waiting when Miller and I reached the surrey. He had his star pinned to his vest and his Colt hanging low on his side.

"Take us to the jail," I said, helping Miller into the back seat, then getting in the surrey myself. When we arrived at the jail, Billy and I did what we could for Miller's leg, washing most of the blood off, and pouring some horse lineament on the wound. "That ought to hold you until morning, then you can hobble up the street and see ole Doc Kelley. You better go early though, before he goes off fishing. Now, Miller, this is what you are being paid for...are you listening to me?" Miller was pretty much sobered up; he nodded and grunted. "We have a prisoner in the back, and from time to time there will be others. Now, your job is to keep them supplied with water, and coffee, and the coffee is only if they behave themselves. Now, around meal time go over to Joe's Café and eat your meal, then bring the prisoner back his lunch...I have already made it okay with the City Council, and you will get paid at the end of every week...did you understand all of that?" Again he nodded, and said yeah. "Now you will notice the keys for the cells are hanging up there on that nail," I pointed and Miller turned his head and looked. "Don't let the prisoner out of his cell under any condition...unless the jail catches on fire."

"What if the prisoner gets choked and needs help?" Miller asked. Bill was standing close, taking in every word, and also waiting on my answer.

"Man! That is the oldest trick in the book, tell him to drink some water and get un-choked."

Billy looked at Miller, and nodded uncertainly, "Just let him die?" Billy asked.

"But what if he really dies?" Miller asked, with a concerned look on his face. Then they both looked at me as I started to the front door of the jail. "

"Then we'll drag him out of his cell and give him or her a decent burial. Let's go, Billy, it's getting late... Miller lock up when we're gone." I could tell Billy was taking this lawman job very seriously and reading everything he could get his hands on. He already knew more than I ever knew about the men that tamed the wild, wild, west.

"Father, do you think Mother will ever ease up on her hate for guns?"

We were nearing the house when Billy asked the question. Again I was lost for words, knowing some questions answer themselves in time.

"Son, I don't believe it is hate for guns... as much as it is the love your mother has for us. I say just give it time and everything will work out."

"Then you are saying Mother may come around to our way of thinking one of these days? You know I don't want to be a doctor or lawyer."

"I know, Billy, but whatever you want to be, be the best at it you can be."

Billy nodded and smiled, "I think I will be the fastest gun in the world."

I couldn't help but laugh as we stepped down from the surrey. "That's a mighty high pedestal you're climbing up on. What about Texas, or the fastest gun in the west?"

Billy was busy unhitching the horse from the surrey. He stopped and looked at me, "Well, Father, if I was the fastest gun in the west, for a nickel more I could go first class, you said it yourself."

"Billy, you know that grown folks sometimes say things that are fables and fairy tales, or old clichés handed down through the years that might be worth being told the second time." I could tell Billy was thinking this over as he stabled the horses and came back where to I was standing.

"In other words, I may ask some questions that you have never dealt with before?"

"That's right, Son, when you were little it seemed I had all the answers, but since you are might-near-grown, I don't want to tell you something that will mislead you in anyway; and I'm sure your mother thinks the same way I do. Did I hear you say that school is out for summer vacation? If so, while I'm gone out of town tomorrow you keep an eye on Miller Davis and the jail."

"Where have you planned to go tomorrow, Father?"

"Didn't I tell you that some cowboy shot his two drinking buddies at the bar at the Silver Slipper tonight? Well, I'm going to ride out early tomorrow and question him, that is if I can find him. According to Miller Davis, the shooter and the two that got shot, are with a trail drive just south of town."

"I sure would like to go with you tomorrow, Father, are you sure you don't want me to ride with you?"

"That would be nice, Son, but you open up the hardware store in the morning and stay until your mother comes over; then you can go on down to the jail. I should be back by then, with any luck at all."

We left the stable and headed for the house. As he and I walked along, I could feel the excitement my son was experiencing...the same as I had felt when I strapped the first Colt on my side, back in Carterville, Illinois, as a young boy. Of course, back then it was only to imagine the wild west and Indians, and stage robbers and outlaws.

Oh yes, I knew my son was fast with a Colt. Like an artist with a brush, or a skilled musician with a violin he wanted to show his skill. The one thing out here in Fort Worth, Texas, when you strap on a side gun...especially if it is tied down to your leg, it's not playing cowboy an Indians. I had already found this out - in Carterville, Illinois...when I was growing up...one died with old age. But out here it's a different story - look at my two deputies and the young bank robbers, dead, all in their thirties.

The next morning I was saddled up and ready to go. I was sitting in Joe's Café when the sun peeped over the few mountains in the back ground, sipping on black coffee and making my game plan for the day. I was into my second cup when Ernest Tilman from the Feed and Seed Store walked in and headed straight for my table like a purple martin to his gourd.

"Pull up a chair and have a seat" I said, as he motioned for the waitress to come over.

"Don't mind if I do." He plopped down and caught my gaze.

"You still got, Butch Parlay, that scum bag that killed your deputy, George Simmons, in jail?"

"I'm afraid so, why do you ask?"

"Well, let me put it this way, Butch and his whole family are a mean bunch of no good cut throats, and you better watch them like a hawk, they are as unpredictable as a Texas twister, and meaner than a sidewinder."

"You know something I don't?" I asked, as the waiter brought his coffee and my breakfast to the table.

"Only if they were gone from the face of this earth, they wouldn't be missed. They owe me money I will never get; none of them work... they rob and rustle cows, and any other way they can make a dishonest dollar."

"In other words, old man Parlay has brought up five sons as sorry and no good as he is?"

"Now, Marshal, you are plowing pretty close to their corn. I couldn't have put it any better myself."

I took the south road out of Fort Worth hoping to see a cloud of dust and a heard of beeves coming my way. Now, if Miller Davis was right, the man I was looking for would be in the midst of this bunch of drovers. It was a beautiful day with not a cloud in the sky; the air was brisk and clean. I stopped my horse, and listening I could hear the popping of the whips and then I saw the cloud of dust on the horizon. Once again a herd of cattle was coming up the old John Chisum Trail, which so many times before millions of hooves had trod, to the stock yard.

Chapter Nine

Billy Has Killed His First Man

I sat on the sideline biding my time, waiting for the fairly large herd to pass me by. I rode over and hailed the chuck wagon down; I knew if anyone could shed some light on the saloon killing last night, the cook could. I rode up close to the chuck wagon and the driver stopped to see what I wanted.

"I'm William Blunt, the U. S. Marshal from Fort Worth, and I'd like to ask you a few questions." The bearded old timer was obliging and pulled up on the reins, with his foot on the brake. He turned loose a mouth full of chewing tobacco juice and caught my gaze.

"What can I do fur ya, young fellow?"

"I'm checking on a man that killed two cowboys in the Silver Slipper last night."

The old man wiped his mouth across his sleeve and slung his head back and forth a time or two as if he had a crick in his neck. "You want to talk to out ramrod, Dick Burke." The old man pointed out a cowboy who was riding drag, and motioned for him to come over where we were. The old man waited for him to ride over.

"Dick, this is the U. S. Marshal from Fort Worth, he wants to ask you a few questions."

The young cowboy nodded and rode closer over to where I was setting.

"I understand you were in the Silver Slipper Saloon last night."

The young cowboy sat up in the saddle and caught hold of his saddle horn. "That's right, Marshal, and I shot two polecats."

The answer kinda took me by surprise and for a minute I was lost for words. "Well I hope you have a good reason, or I'm going to have to take you in for murder this morning."

The young cowboy looked at the old man sitting on the chuck wagon. The old man nodded as is to say, go ahead and tell the Marshal what happened.

"Marshal, we left south Texas two months ago with this herd, and the owner Mr. Caraway. The two men I killed last night were Allan Young and his cousin, Buford Young. They hired on when we first started this trail drive. I tried to tell Mr. Caraway they were trouble and not to hire them, but, we needed to move the cows and Mr. Caraway needed the money to pay off a loan to the bank, in order to save his ranch. Now, Marshal, both Allen and Buford approached me last week and tried to get me to go along with them, to steal the money from Mr. Caraway when the cows were sold, and then go with them to Canada. I never paid them any mind, thinking they were just blowing hot air...but when they killed Mr. Caraway yesterday morning that was a little much, and I looked them up last night and shot them."

"You said they killed Mr. Caraway, can you prove that?" He looked back at the old man sitting on the chuck wagon.

"You tell 'em, Gabby."

The old man turned loose of a mouth full of tobacco spit, and again wiped his mouth on this shirt sleeve. "We have an eyewitness that seen 'em do it. It was before chow yesterday when Allen and Buford come riding in here and said Mr. Caraway's horse must have been spooked and threw him... and he must have hit his head on a rock, killing him. We believed what they had said until Chico, a Mexican boy that worked for Mr. Caraway, was hunting for a deer and seen them hit him in the head with a big rock and killed him. Chico said he was hid and they never saw him in the brush."

"Is Chico a reliable source to believe?" I asked.

"Marshal, if Chico tells you a chicken dips snuff, you can look under her wing for the snuff can."

"You think you boys can scrape up a few dollars to give to the undertaker to hire someone to dig a few holes on boot-hill, when you get to town?" I asked.

"You tell the undertaker to go ahead and bury the remains and I will personally settle up when we get this herd to town."

As I whipped my horse around to leave, I wondered if there was anything else I could do. All I knew was that the young cowboy had saved the town a trial and a few dollars by being his own judge and jury; but, taking the law into your own hands is not the thing to do. As I started back to town I was empty handed, but felt that justice had been done - maybe not an eye for an eye - but the two greedy cowboys got what they deserved.

It was going on twelve o'clock when I rode back in town. I didn't need to look at my watch; my stomach was giving me the word. I also had another gut feeling that was strange; it was like something I had never felt before...kind of a sickening feeling. It being a week day, the mornings were never busy, so I decided to go by the jail and check on things before going on over to Joe's Café for lunch. As I rode down Main Street, it was like a ghost town; some store owners had actually closed up shop and put a closed sign in the window. That gut feeling was getting even worse. The only living creature I had seen, since riding into town, was a man standing in front of the jail, propped up on a shovel. I tied up my mount and walked over to the man; I recognized him to be Harris Spick, one of the men that Craig Watson, our undertaker, used to dig graves.

"Good day, sir, what is going on?" I asked.

He never moved. "You may need to talk with Miller Davis, he's been waiting on you to get back."

I don't mind telling you my heart nearly stopped; I became weak in the knees...if something had happened to my son, Billy, I would never forgive myself. I stepped up on the porch and slowly turned the door knob, expecting to hear the worst.

I caught Miller's gaze as quick as I walked into the jail. "Its Billy isn't it?" I slowly asked. When Miller nodded I nearly lost my breath. Miller was sitting at the desk. I made it to a chair and sat down.

"Tell me what happened." It took all I could do to keep from busting out in tears.

Miller took a sip of his coffee and started his story: "I guess Billy had finished up his work over at the hardware store. He said you said he could come over here and help me the rest of the day. He had his star on his vest and his peacemaker hanging low on his side, tied down. He asked how Butch was doing in the back. If I remember, he went to the kitchen and came back drinking a cup of coffee. It was then he and I heard horses ride up. We looked at each other and shook our heads, then a voice outside yelled, 'Marshal! Marshal, I need to see you out here!' Miller stopped. I didn't know if I really wanted to hear the rest of the story; I didn't say anything but sat there spellbound. Miller took another big swig of his coffee, a deep breath, and went on with his story.

"Marshal Blunt...you have a son you can be proud of, I saw a professional at work this morning. Billy quickly put his cup of coffee down, flipped the thong off the hammer of his Colt, and drew it out of his holster and spun the cylinder to see if it was fully loaded. As he stepped to the front door he slowly dropped his pistol back in his low hanging gun belt, and pulled the jail door wide open. I jumped up and was standing behind Billy. 'Can I help you Mr. Parlay? The Marshal isn't here right now, it's just me and Miller Davis.' Well that's all it took, Marshal, Old Man Parlay and his three sons went to laughing. 'The Marshal has left a snotty nosed kid and a old drunk to keep my boy in jail...Raymond, you and Clint go inside and get your brother, Butch.' Well, to make a long story short, they slid out of the saddle, and here they come. When the first brother reached Billy, he more or less stiff-armed the Parlay boy, shoving him backwards, and the other brother tried to catch him. It was kind of comical in a way, both fell off the porch in the dirt. Now, Marshal, the boy he shoved jumped up and went for his pistol...and Marshal, he had it out of his holster, when Billy drew his Colt and put a bullet dead center between his eyes. Well, the other boy looked down and saw what happened. 'You've killed my brother,' he cried out, and went for his pistol... and you can believe it or not, but Billy waited until he drew it out of his holster, then Billy did a repeat performance, and gave him a third eye. Well, old man Parlay saw what had happened in a split second, and he screamed at the brother still sitting on his horse,'Kill that boy, Arnold!' With four chunks of lead still in Billy's Colt it was no contest, he peeled him out of his saddle like you would peel an apple." I was on the edge of my chair listening to every word, wondering what had happened next. "It just so happened that old man Parlay wasn't even wearing a pistol. 'I'll show you a thing or two, boy,' old man Parlay yelled. Billy was still standing on the porch, with two slugs still waiting. Old Man Parlay leaned way over and drew a Henry out of a boot on the horse sitting next to him, and as he swung around he breached a cartridge into the magazine; this was his second mistake of the day. Billy emptied his Colt into Old Man Parlay's chest, and he was dead when he hit the ground. You've got you some brave boy for a son, Marshal Blunt."

I thanked Miller and started on to the house to check on things there. I also thanked the man standing out front; he had done a splendid job covering the blood stains, and making the place more presentable. I placed my boot in the stirrup and caught the saddle horn to get on my mount. I leaned against the saddle and for a minute or two I began to think: 'Was Elizabeth right? Have guns brought our family to this? My only son, sixteen years old, has taken four lives, a father and three sons...what will the implications be? What will the church folks say? Will the family of the deceased hold a grudge and try to get revenge? I guess time will tell.' I threw my leg over the saddle and started toward the stable behind my house.

I slowly unsaddled my horse and threw the sweaty blanket over the fence to dry out. Thoughts were bombarding my mind as I began to curry my horse. My horse always seemed to enjoy my straightening the hair out on his back. I made sure the trough had ample water as I turned my horse out in a small pasture to graze.

Elizabeth was in the kitchen when I came through the back door. "Hello, Dear, I'm home." I trained my ear but heard nothing. I think sometimes silence is the best teacher, but today I wasn't sure. Maybe she hadn't heard me, "Hello, Dear, I'm home." As I neared her she stood with her back turned to me. I had no idea what I was going to say or do, for that matter. Again I was lost for words. I guess I deserved what was coming... 'I told you so', she could say...or, 'now you know why I'm opposed to guns'.

I touched Elizabeth on the shoulder and she turned to face me. I saw a woman I had never seen before, no powder, no paint, but big tears were streaming down her face, and had soaked the front of her dress.

Her lips began to move, but nothing was coming out. She cleared her throat and held her arms toward me. "Hold me, Darling, I need you." I pulled off my hat and threw it on the kitchen table alongside Billy's deputy star, and his gun rigging all rolled up. "I thank God my son was spared from that bunch of wicked men, it could have been you William!" My wife was more passionate than I had ever seen her.

"Where is Billy?" I asked.

"He is in his room, reading his Bible, our pastor is on his way over to see us." I let Elizabeth loose and turned toward Billy's bedroom. "William, what is done is done, remember that," she said, as I walked away from her. Billy's door was closed when I eased down the hall to his room. Again, I was lost for words; I knew one thing, depression and sadness, and the devil, can bring an awful pain to a body after killing his first man.

I lightly tapped on the door. "It's open, come on in." My wife was right, Billy was sitting over by a window, reading his Bible.

We both focused our gaze, but said nothing for a second or two. "I'm proud of you son, you did exactly what I would have done if I had been at the jail this morning." A slight smile appeared on his face. "You know that being big enough to use a pistol means you must be big enough to suffer the consequences."

Billy nodded his head. "I've read all about that, Father and I sure don't want to fall into that pit of doom and gloom." Billy held up his Bible. "That devil has done been here and gone, Father." I knew that my sixteen year old son was now grown.

"What did your mother say when you told her what you had done this morning?"

Billy closed his Bible and straightened up. "After hearing the whole story, tears came to her eyes, and she said, 'Your father taught you well, Son, how to grow up out West.'" Tears came to my eyes knowing that I had done something my wife approved of.

"Why is your gun lying on the kitchen table?" I asked. "Don't tell me you are giving up this easily."

Billy smiled and shook his head. "Mother said before I put it back on she wanted to pray over it, to be a blessing to folks in our town and not a deadly tool."

The implications of this fiasco, as our pastor called it, was uncalled for... especially by a sixteen year old boy. He began to imply that Billy should have stepped aside and let the father take his son; it would have been better than having the blood of four innocent men on his hands. In all the years Elizabeth and I had been married, this was the first time I ever saw her get in the face of someone.

"Now you wait one minute, Pastor Wallace...you have called my son a murderer, this was not innocent blood, they were breaking the law."

"Mrs. Blunt, I can tell we disagree on how things are run, but Billy will need to go through some counseling before he can come back to my church." I was seated facing both the preacher and Elizabeth, and at that remark she started rising from her chair. I knew the pastor's evaluation of Billy actions was harsh and asinine, but what Elizabeth did put icing on the cake.

She politely pranced to the front door of our big living room and swung the door wide open. She stood very straight and held her head slightly back. "You leave my house right this minute." Elizabeth ordered.

"But...Mrs. Blunt," the preacher hesitated.

"Right now! Don't let my husband have to throw you out."

Well, needless to say, when word got around that my wife had ordered the preacher out of our house, this divided the church of course, the preacher had his side of the story as well...but still many left the church. Elizabeth and I became very close. I wondered what made the change in her. Was it the week I was out of town and shot the eight Indians and nearly got killed myself, or was it Billy's heroic act at the jail - upholding the law?

It would be some time later I would really know, what made the change in my wife. Maybe a change I was not ready for at the time.

Chapter Ten

Billy Gets Shot

In the next few weeks... good or sad to say, Billy became a legend in his own time. In the still of night we were all sleeping, when we heard a crashing sound in our living room. We lit a lamp and rushed to see what the disturbance might have been. It was plain to see - a big rock lying in the middle of the living room floor, with a note attached. We gathered that it had been thrown through our big, front room window. I held the lamp while Elizabeth read the words on the attached note. 'Billy boy! the Parlay family had lots of friends; we will get even soon.'

When Elizabeth finished reading she looked at Billy who was standing in the circle. "Go in my bedroom and get my Bible!" Now since we've married I have seen Elizabeth do some strange things, but nothing like this. Billy was back in a flash. He handed his mother the Bible and stepped back. As sure as I'm telling this story, Elizabeth laid her Bible on a drum table sitting right in front of the busted window; and then she laid the rock right on top of the Bible. Billy looked at me and I at him, not knowing what Elizabeth would do next.

Elizabeth then laid her open hand on top of the rock. I noticed her body jerk several times, and then she began to speak. "In the Name of Jesus of Nazareth, the Name that is above all Names, I rebuke this rock and the hands that threw it into our living room window." Then she became limp as if virtue had gone from her body, and she turned and slowly made her way back to her bedroom.

It was told by young Dorothy Macon, that a cousin of Butch Parlay's stopped in at Joe's Café the next morning for coffee, before going to work. He told her he threw a rock into Billy's house to scare him to death. It just so happened that same day he and a friend were cutting logs for a sawmill near by. As we were told, the two were sawing down a big tall pine tree with a sharp cross-cut saw. Now, according to the friend, as the tree began to fall, the wind changed directions and the huge pine began to fall backward onto the cousin, who couldn't get out of the path of destruction in time, and he was crushed to death.

A few days later, Billy was coming home from the hardware store. It was late and nearly dark, when he heard a shot ring out. He couldn't even tell where the shot came from...from a back alley, the edge of the woods, or the top of a building. All that Billy knew was that he had been shot, because he felt a sting in his arm. Many others heard the shot and came running to give assistance. Billy ducked down behind a huge watering trough until the coast was clear, and the shooter was scared off.

You might say the kin and friends of the Parlay family were now using other mean; the rock throwing and scare tactics were not working. Billy was still going about his job as if nothing was wrong. It just so happened the Circuit Judge arrived on the stage that day and Butch Parlay's trial was set for the next...what a coincidence for the shooting this evening. The wound wasn't all that bad, but it could have been fatal. The shooter wasn't just shooting to nick Billy's arm, by no means.

It was for sure, bad news around Fort Worth in the early days, traveled like wild fire in dry sage brush. Elizabeth had already heard the news about Billy getting shot, but didn't know where or how badly. Well, here she came running, to meet Billy and the men bringing him over to the house. She was still praying when she reached him. Now, seeing it was only a flesh wound, she thanked the men and said she would take over now and see him on home. After she and Billy were safely inside the house, and Billy's arm was attended to, Elizabeth brought the Bible to her son to read. "Read this while I'm finishing up the evening meal. Your father will be home soon!"

Now, let me let Billy tell this part of the story...

The Bible was already turned to the book and page of the Bible she wanted me to read. And with nothing more to do but wait on supper and my father to get home, I gently accepted the Bible from Mother and started reading.

I noticed it was the Book of Job which I had read a few years back, when I had the urge to read through the Bible in a year. This time I'll take my time and concentrate on what the Lord and my mother would like me to know and understand, I thought. I had read the first two chapters and started on the third when Mother came into the living room where I was and sat down. I looked up and caught her gaze.

"I'm waiting on the bread to bake." Mother said, straightening her white apron.

"I'm starting on the third chapter, Mother," I explained, as I looked down at the Bible.

"Oh, that's enough, Son, the first two chapters are enough for now. What have you read so far?" Her question took me by surprise, it was one of those spur of the moment things, and I had to think for a minute.

"Well, for one thing, the Lord is talking to the devil."

"Yes, that's right, go on."

"It appears that Satan is trying to corrupt the lives of all the people here on earth."

"That's good, Billy," Mother answered all excited, "do go on."

I thought for a second before I continued. "Well, as I read, God wants to know why Satan hadn't tried to make Job sin." I was hoping I gave Mother the answer she wanted.

"Very good, Billy, now why do you think that the devil didn't try to attack Job?" I remembered reading about that.

"God had a hedge built all around Job that the devil couldn't penetrate; isn't that right?"

Mother gave me a big smile. "Yes, that is right, and that is exactly what I'm going to do for you." Just before Mother got all carried away with whatever she was going to do, I heard Father come in the back door.

"Is anyone home, where is everybody?"

"We're in the living room, Dear, and if you would… take the pone of cornbread out of the oven for me!" Mother yelled out. I heard the oven door squeak, and shortly Father came walking in where mother and I were. I could tell he was completely in the dark on what happened to me.

"What's the matter with your arm, Son?" Father asked, stepping closer to take a better look.

"I've been shot."

"Been shot?" Father blurted out.

"Yes, he has been shot!" Mother exclaimed, "but it will be the last time a bullet will ever touch my son's body."

"How can you guarantee that, Elizabeth?" Father asked.

"I can't, but God can; let me read you this in Job chapter one, starting with verse six: *'Now there was a day when the sons of God came to present themselves before the Lord, and Satan came also among them. And the Lord said unto Satan, Whence comest thou? Then Satan answered the Lord, and said, From going to and fro in the earth, and from walking up and down in it. And the Lord said unto Satan, Hast thou considered My servant Job, that there is none like him in the earth, a perfect and an upright man, one that feareth God, and escheweth evil? Then Satan answered the Lord, and said, Doth Job fear God for naught? Hast not thou made an hedge about him, and about his house, and about all that he hath on every side? thou hast blessed the work of his hands, and his substance is increased in the land.'* Now, William, take Billy's hand. We're going to pray a hedge around Billy, that the devil's bullets will never touch him ever again."

I looked at Father, and he at me, as we all held hands, and Mother started praying. "Oh hear me now Lord, in Jesus' Name, You build a hedge around my son, Billy. You build it tall and thick, where no bullet can ever penetrate his body, this I pray in Jesus' Name."

"Is that it?" my father asked, turning loose of my hand.

"That it!" Mother said, getting up, "God is not deaf, neither do you have to beg, if you are His child...are you all ready to eat dinner?"

As I sat eating supper, 'course Mother called it dinner, I was thinking: Was I never to get shot again? This is far out! Can God do something like that? I'm sure Father had an issue with that as well. He soon finished eating, pushed his plate back, and picked up his cup of coffee.

"Elizabeth, and you as well, Billy, I want you to be in prayer about a problem that is brewing north and south of Fort Worth, and it is about to come to a head." Father took a swallow of his coffee, cleared his throat, and wiped his mouth on a napkin. "You all know Don York, we call 'em Big Don, he has a ranch just south of town; and he is one of my best friends. You remember, Elizabeth, he was here when we first moved to Fort Worth. He helped us get established with his moral support, and introducing us to the right people." Father took another sip of his coffee and looked at Mother. "Well, to make a long story short, he is about to get in trouble with the law, and this will involve our friendship." I had finished my meal and was dying to know what was the problem with Mr. Big Don.

This is when Mother spoke up, "Surely, William, this problem as you call it... has a solution."

"You would think so, but Big Don is being bull-headed and won't listen to reason. You know, Elizabeth, he has the biggest spread in Texas, but all the land his cattle is grazing on is not his...can't you see?"

"Yes, I see," Mother acknowledged. "It was the same way in church before we stopped going, it was his way or the highway."

"You might say Big Don has overstepped his bounds this time; a family that has moved in on the south side of what he calls 'his ranch', but doesn't have a legal title too."

"So."

"So the family has a deed to the property, legal and proper, according to the land office."

"I'd sure hate to be in your boots on this decision, Father," I said, excusing myself from the table.

"Billy is right, what are you going to do? You don't even know these strangers that have moved in on Big Don's grazing land."

I stopped and turned around facing Mother. "Mother, it was the same as when I shot those four men; they were breaking the law the same as Big Don is doing."

"Well, I certainly hope your father doesn't go out there and shoot 'im."

Father started laughing and laid his hand over on Mother's arm. "No danger in that, but somebody needs to knock some sense into his stubborn ol' hard head, before he rides out there and harasses the strangers."

"Have you met the family that has moved out there on Big Don's so called range?" Elizabeth asked, starting to stack the dirty plates.

"Yes, I have...the O'Reilly's... and they seem to be fine upstanding folks with good Christian morals. The old man said that God guided him to that land and he and his family weren't going to be run off. And if you saw the size of his three sons... I wouldn't want to tangle with them. Of course, Big Don has them outnumbered, and more guns, too."

"And I guess you are going to be right in the thick of things?" Mother asked .as she walked over to the sink.

"I have to, Elizabeth, it is my job to uphold the law, even if these sod-busters are going to start farming the land, it is their God given right. I tried to explain to Big Don he has more land than he can look after now."

"You care if I ride along with you in the morning, Father?"

He looked at Mother and she smiled, "I don't mind, it's you that I'm worried about, not Billy."

"Well if that don't beat all, Billy, your mother prayed for you and left me out."

"William, I didn't do it on purpose, I just thought you were big enough to pray for yourself."

"That might be true, but I have more faith in your prayers than I do my own." Father said, moving over to where Mother was at the sink.

She quickly dried her hands and caught Father by both hands, and went to praying. Mother prayed for him and his job and his safe return tomorrow. I even felt the Spirit where I was standing in the door way.

The next morning Father and I woke up bright and early. to a beautiful day and a good breakfast, as we headed for the stable back of our house I asked, "You think there will be trouble this morning, Father?"

"Well, I hope not, but if Big Don comes down where the family is setting up camp, and tries to run them off, there will be trouble." We finished saddling our horses and made sure our Henrys were in our scabbard. "Isn't that your mother coming down here?" Father asked.

"I believe it is, this is very unusual." We stood waiting, not knowing what to expect when Mother walked up.

"I was praying after you two left out of the kitchen, and I saw something in a vision I didn't like." Well...I don't mind telling you, which kinda floored both me and father.

"Don't look so surprised, it didn't have anything to do with either of you."

I looked at Father, wondering if this was a good idea, we were kinda butting in on someone else's rat killing, but I didn't say anything.

"Can you tell us, Elizabeth, what you saw in your vision? We might not need to go this morning," Father commented.

"As I said, it doesn't have anything to do with you or Billy, it's as if God is going to take care of this situation between Big Don and the new family, and you and Billy will be onlookers."

"I hope you're right, Darling, I would hate to lose friendship with Big Don over a thing like this."

"All I know is, God has spoken and He can't lie." Mother turned and started back up the path toward the house. Father led his horse and walked with Mother, with his arm around her waist. He stood and waited until she was in the house before he mounted his horse. I was already mounted and caught up with Father and we rode together.

"What do you think, Father?"

"Think about what, Son?"

"About what Mother saw and said?"

"Some of that I take with a grain of salt, but we will soon know."

And now I'll let Billy rest and tell this part of the story...

We had a pretty good ride before reaching our destination. As Billy and I neared the camp site of the strangers, we could see they were busy about their chores and seemed not to have a worry in the world. But I still say if they knew Big Don like I knew him to be, this family would be boarded up and ready to fight...what's so bad - they don't believe in guns and probably don't even have one that will shoot in the first place.

"I see y'all are hard at it this fine morning" I said to the father of the clan.

"That we are, that we are laddie, we want to get a cabin built before winter."

"You do know that Big Don is coming out this morning to talk to you, or have you forgot?"

"Oh no, we haven't forgot, Marshal, it's just we have other things to do with our lives than to keep up with Big Don."

"But you know he could cause trouble for you."

"Oh yes, but we have the law on our side; isn't that why you are here this morning?"

I thought to myself, if this old Irishman knew what was in store for him this morning, law, or no law, he would be long gone. But it was good to see someone with a backbone still left in this old world.

"You do know that we are no match for Big Don and his dozen hired gunslingers...don't you?"

"Marshal, you should know as well as I, the side of the law always wins out."

"Yes, I do, you know that, and I know that, but does Big Don know that? You do know you can be right, but dead right?"

"We shall see, my good man. I see Big Don and his merry men coming on the horizon."

I turned in the saddle and sure enough I saw Big Don and his men in the distance. Billy and I was still sitting in the saddle when Big Don rode in. His men stayed in the back, while Big Don took the lead and rode closer.

"I thought I told you and your family to be off my property by this morning. Did you not hear me, are is it you bunch of Irishman can't understand plain English?"

"Oh, we heard you, Matey, but who are you to tell us to get off of our own land?" I could tell that statement made Big Don a little huffy.

"You listen to me, you old coot, I have run my cattle in this valley for twenty five years. I have put up with rustlers, Indians, clodhoppers, and sod busters, and even a few sheep herders during that time, and now you tell me I don't own this land?"

Billy and I sat in the distance and listened.

"That is right sir, you never filed a claim on this land, according to the law."

"What does the law know about my land I raise cattle on?"

"The law of the land knows you don't own this fertile valley, and if you and your men will excuse me I have work to do."

I could almost see the smoke rising in Big Don as he looked back at his men behind him; he knew they would do anything he asked of them. "What's that settin' over there on the table where the girl is seated?"

The daughter was sitting at a small table close to the covered wagon. the mother was in the wagon looking out the back.

"It is an alarm clock, sir, what about it?" Mr. O'Reilly answered.

"Ask her what time is it?"

"The man wants to know what time it is, Catherine." The girl turned the clock around where Big Don could see it. He rode up a little closer to the table, and stretched his neck looking.

"Its five minutes until nine o'clock, Mr. O'Reilly, you've got five minutes to start packing to leave, or me and my boys will start shooting and tearing up your camp."

Billy and I were sitting within hearing distance, but in the back ground not saying a word. A minute or so passed and no one had moved, and the clock was still ticking.

Soon Billy leaned over toward me and quietly asked, "Father, isn't there anything we can do?"

"Not until he breaks a law!"

"But he is breaking the law by trespassing on Mr. O'Reilly's property. There are 'no trespassing' signs up."

I was looking right at Big Don when he took a handkerchief out of his back pocket and wiped his face and yelled out, "You and your bunch has less than one minute to clear out!" He dropped his handkerchief to the ground and put both of his hands on his chest. He fell forward out of the saddle to the ground and never moved or took another breath of God's free air.

I guess I was the first one there at the body; Big Don had no pulse and no sign of breathing. His men, all but two or three, came up to the body, but said nothing. I knew Big Don's foreman, Mack Browder, and I started talking to him.

"You know that Big Don was my best friend?"

"I knew that, Marshal, and me, along with all the other men, didn't want to do what the boss man wanted us to do. This old Irishman has rights, same as we do. Besides I checked it all out the same day Big Don checked on this land; it belongs to this family free and clear."

"Mack, if you don't mind, I am going to see if Mr. O'Reilly won't let me use his buckboard to carry Big Don's body back to the morgue in Fort Worth. I don't think it's fitting to tie him across a horse like some outlaw."

"That's right neighborly of you, Marshal. I'll tell his new wife where Big Don's body is, and what happened to him this morning, though it won't make much difference to her one way or the other."

That comment caused me to ask another question. "Is there some division in the marriage I don't know about?"

I could tell that Mack Browder was somewhat reluctant to answer the question. "Look Marshal let us let the dead rest in peace, and I will say no more...but Nancy...his new wife, spent more time in the bunkhouse than she did in the big house."

"Did she have a preference or favorite?" I asked.

"Oh yes, excluding me, just the cowboys that wore spurs!"

I knew this question and answer conversation was over, and left Mack to converse with the other men that had come with Big Don. Mr. O'Reilly said he, and his wife Daisy, needed some supplies from town, and would be more than happy to take the body to the morgue.

I knew that Big Don had a son and daughter living in Houston who needed to be sent a telegram, as soon as possible. After leaving the telegraph office, and before he and I rode to our stable I could tell Billy was about to burst to tell me something. or to ask a question.

"Okay, you've been awfully quiet, what's on your mind?" Billy rode over a little closer to me and looked all around. "Do you think Mother actually saw Big Don in that vision she told us about this morning?" This question sort of set me back in the saddle, so they say.

"Billy, I don't believe so. Don't you believe if she knew she would have told us so we would have been expecting Big Don to have that heart attack?"

"You know, Father, I was thinking along those very lines, and what about the boy that threw the rock through our window? You know he met with a fatal accident the next day. You reckon Mother saw a tree fall on Butch's cousin?"

"Oh, no, it's just a generic type of vision, an it's like one size fits all," I said to Billy.

"You're saying God leaves out calling names, and we know something bad is going to happen, but we don't know what?"

"I believe you hit the nail on the head, Son. I couldn't have answered it better."

"Father, when we get the horses unsaddled and rubbed down, will you let me be the first to tell Mother what happened today?"

"Sure. I don't mind, you saw and heard the whole thing."

Billy finished way before I did, and was waiting for me to walk into the kitchen with him. Elizabeth was waiting lunch for us. I didn't realize it was this late; it was almost one o'clock.

Chapter Eleven

Billy Was Excited

"Mother, you aren't going to believe what happened after Father and I rode into Mr. O'Reilly's camp this morning!"

Mother stopped what she was doing, turned toward me, and put her hands on her hips. "And why wouldn't I believe what you are going to tell me?" I looked at Father, he nodded as if to say, go ahead and tell her.

"Mother, it was nip and tuck for a minute or two... then it was just like you prophesied this morning. Mr. Big Don gave the O'Reilly family five minutes to pack up and leave, or he was gonna start shooting the camp up, and you know somebody would have gotten hurt." I had sat down at the table with a cup of coffee; while Billy told the story...Elizabeth's eyes were getting bigger and bigger. "Mother, there was an alarm clock on a table where the girl was. It said five minutes to nine o'clock...and Mother, when Mr. Big Don started to give word for his men to start shooting, he grabbed his chest and fell forward to the ground, dead as a door nail. I didn't check 'im, but Father did. As you said, Mother, God certainly took care of that situation."

"Wait one minute, Billy, though I predicted something would happen, and I am a child of God...God had nothing to do with Big Don having a heart attack and dying."

"But I thought you said God was going to intervene, and me and father weren't going to be involved."

"I did, Son, but know this, God doesn't give people heart attacks; Big Don brought this all on himself. What the devil meant for bad, God used for good. And you or your father weren't involved, just as in my vision."

"Mother, I just about don't understand what you're saying. But it all worked out the way you said, anyhow."

As we sat eating our late lunch, Father began to talk of another incident brewing, just north of Fort Worth. "One could say it's like a volcano just fixin' to erupt...and it'll need to be dealt with, in time."

"Is it something we ought to pray about soon?" Mother asked, seeming very concerned. I was also anxious to know what it was all about.

"You all are familiar with Walter King's big cattle spread north of here."

"Are you talking about the King that has been in the news, here lately?" Mother asked.

"One and the same, he has been just one-step-dodging the law for years, that is what I was told when I first took this job as U. S. Marshal. I understand he is running a sanctuary for outlaws. One of the men that work for Walter King was killed the other day up in Gainesville, Texas, trying to rob a store."

"What happened, William?" Mother asked.

"I don't know the whole story, Dear, but evidently he didn't figure the store owner kept a loaded shotgun under the counter."

"Did the store owner kill the man, Father?" Billy asked, moving over close to me. I knew the next question Billy was going to ask me.

"Father, do you mind if I ride with you when you go up to Gainesville?"

"Billy, it will probably be after the funeral of Big Don, and I don't know when that will be...tomorrow, I hope."

"What was that I heard about his wife, Father?"

"You weren't supposed to hear that, Billy!"

"Now, William ,what is this all about?" asked Elizabeth.

"After Big Don's first wife died last year, he married some slut that worked in a saloon, from Houston."

"Now, William, you shouldn't say words like that around Billy." Father looked a little put out.

"I think it sounds better than a plain, old whore, don't you, Elizabeth?"

"Father, what's the difference between a slut and a plain old whore?"

Elizabeth shrugged her shoulder and twisted her mouth. "You explain to him, Elizabeth, I have work to do down at the jail." I eased up and started for the back door as I heard Elizabeth trying to explain.

"I don't know if there is much difference between the two... all I know is they both will bust hell wide open if they don't change their wicked ways.

On my way to the jail I went by the telegraph office, where I had three telegrams waiting. Then I moseyed to the newspaper office and found I had two new "Wanted' posters that had come in, also; seems they all had to do with Walter King, directly or indirectly. I knew the writing was on the wall, and something had to be done before things grew worse, if that is possible; one man was dead already, and no telling what was in store next.

I wanted to get by the feed and seed store before it closed, to ask Mr. Tillman a few questions. I thought if anybody knew what was going on in and around Fort Worth, he would know. Mr. Tillman, a long time resident of the town, had seen lots of water run under the bridge, as they say. I quickly made tracks around and got my rat-killing done, and headed on over to the Feed and Seed store. I found Mr. Tillman taking inventory, and felt reluctant to bother him with my frivolous questions.

"I need to talk with you, if you can spare the time." He looked around and saw who I was and laid his clip-board down, and stuck his pencil back in his shirt pocket.

"Evening, Marshal, I need to talk with you also, how about a cup of fresh coffee while we jaw a spell?"

"I don't mind if I do."

I followed Mr. Tillman to the back of the store where he had a small wood heater and a blue granite coffee pot. "I hope you take it black, my cow is dried up and I found out sugar don't set well with me."

"Black is fine with me."

He filled two tin cups and offered one to me. "We might as well take the load off our boots," he said, then motioned for me to sit down in a straw-bottomed straight chair.

"I hate to keep you from your work, Mr. Tillman. But I knew if anybody in this town knew anything, it would be you."

"Well, I don't know about that; but mine was one of the first places of business in Fort Worth, Texas."

"For starters, Mr. Tillman, there were things that went on in this town, before I took the job as U. S. Marshal, which I don't know about. Has it been swept 'under the rug', as they say, and just now coming out in the open?"

Mr. Tillman took a swig of his coffee and caught my gaze. "Marshal, you need to be more specific."

"The last sheriff, how did he get killed? And what do you know about Walter King, who has a big ranch north of here."

"You might near answered your own question, Marshal."

"You're saying Walter King might have something to do with his killing?"

"Well that was the rumor for a long time, but couldn't be proved...and who was here that was going to challenge him?"

"I see what you mean, Mr. Tillman, but I think the chickens have come home to roost, if you get my drift?"

"Then you are saying... you now have proof that Walter King is involved in some shady transactions? That is not news to me, Marshal, I've known that for years, but I didn't want to stir up more trouble in town."

"What would you do if you were me, would you confront him?" I asked, hoping to get some valid advice from a older head.

"If I wanted to get killed, that's exactly what I would do," he began laughing, "You might want to let that sleeping dog lie, until he causes trouble in this town again."

I took the reward posters out of my pocket and unfolded them. "Do you know either of these men?"

Mr. Tillman pushed his specks up on this nose and cocked his head one way an' then the other. "This 'un I do, he works for Walter King."

"What about this man?" I showed Mr. Tillman the other wanted poster, and waited. I noticed the expression on his face changed, and he started shaking his head.

"Marshal, I've had a run in with this man, he's meaner than a snake, he'll shoot you at the drop of a hat; and while you are not looking he'll drop the hat."

"You said you've had a run in with this man?" I asked, pointing at the poster.

"Well...not exactly him, but his wife, or girlfriend, she works over at the saloon." I looked up toward the street.

"Which one? We've got three or four, and it looks like more coming each day."

"I think the Silver Slipper, I don't patronize those types of places, as you well know. And my wife thinks they all need to be put out of business."

"I'm afraid that Elizabeth feels the same way, but there is little you and I can do about it now. I understand it's a free country... you sell your seed and feed, and they sell their beer and rot-gut whiskey; and I try to keep the peace. Sad to say, I'm selling my gun and my life."

Mr. Tillman looked somewhat disappointed, to say the least. "Do you look at your job in that respect, Marshal?"

"Yes, I do now, but not when I first took the U. S. Marshal's job. You know Governor Davis talked me into it. Even Elizabeth was against it at first, and probably wished I would quit right now, before I get killed."

"Marshal, I was under the impression you liked the Marshal's job," Mr. Tillman said.

"I hope this doesn't come as a surprise to you, but I haven't had one decent night's sleep since I took this damn job, pardon my French. Do you know what it's like to take a life?" Mr. Tillman started shaking his head. "Well, I do, let me tell you. I moved out here from back east and started a business as a God-fearing man. You look now - I'm hated by half of the town, and scared to go out at night, afraid I'll be shot in the back by some trigger happy cowboy, trying to make a name for himself."

"Are you planning on giving up the job?"

"No! A lot of things I am, but a quitter I'm not... I'll see this job through, if it kills me."

"Marshal, we don't want that to happen to you."

"Neither does my wife or son. What about the City Council hiring me a good deputy?"

"Why don't you put your son, Billy, on the payroll? From what I have seen and heard, he can hold his own with the best of 'em."

"If you don't mind, let's leave my son, Billy, out of this conservation. He's in enough trouble, shooting that Parlay mob a while back, and not nearly as much trouble, as he's in with his mother."

I made it on over to my hardware store and made sure that Lewis Brady had everything under control; he was a new man that Elizabeth had hired full time, and from what I was told, he was doing a great job. She said he was as honest as the day was long, and gave him full reign of the store. I noticed Lewis had taken in two pistols to be fixed, and since I was gone most of the time, I decided to give them a looking over. There was no one in the store at the time, and my hired help stood looking on as I sat down at my desk and picked up one of the pistols. It had been neglected by its owner, and rust had overcome its shooting ability.

"Marshal Blunt, I'm pretty good fixing guns. I can take care of this 'un for you if you have something else to do." Lewis Brady looked on as I reached for the other pistol. "Marshal Blunt, I believe you will find it has a broken firing pin," Lewis said, starting to disassemble the first pistol.

"You are right, Lewis, I do have other things to do, just fix both of them pistols in your spare time, and charge accordingly."

I left Lewis to wait on the customers and lock up, when the time came to close. I moseyed on to the Silver Slipper Saloon to check on the man pictured on the Wanted poster. If I had known then what I would find out later I would have taken Mr. Tillman's advice and let this sleeping dog lie. It was getting about time for the beer guzzlers and party goers to start gathering up for their time of fun, frolic and fellowship, as you know misery loves company.

I eased over to where Justin Mann was standing; he was the new bartender now. The other had caught a stray bullet last week, which sent him to boot hill. The sad part, didn't anyone see who did the shooting.

"Can I serve you, Marshal?" he asked, wiping off the bar with a rag. I took out the two reward posters, unfolded them, and handed him one to look at.

"Blade Phillips, the name is right, but the resemblance is not much like him," Justin remarked, handing me the poster back.

I thought for a second and asked. "Now, what gives you that impression, my good man?" He picked up a shot glass and began to shine it up. "Well he's sitting right over there at the table with Betty Lou Corbet."

I quickly looked at the reward poster and back at Blade Phillip., The bartender was right, the resemblance was way off. I thanked the bartender for his help and eased over to where the couple were sitting, minding their own business.

"You Blade Phillips, and work for Walter King?"

"That's right, Marshal, pull up a chair and join me and Betty Lou. She don't mind, do you, Baby?"

I pulled a empty chair out from the table, and sat down.

"Now, Marshal, what can me and this sweet thing do for you?" He put his arm around the dance hall girl and pulled her up close to him, and waited for my reply. I pulled the Wanted poster out of my shirt pocket and passed it across the table. He stretched out his hand and took it, and began to open it up very carefully, not saying a word.

"Is that you, Darling?" the girl asked, putting her face up close to his face. "It sure doesn't look like you, does it?"

"The picture doesn't matter, Sir, did you rob the bank in Orville, as the poster says you did?" I could tell I wasn't as popular as I was when I first sat down.

He folded up the poster and handed it back to me. "I don't know anything about this Wanted poster."

"Then I'm sure this matter can be cleared up in no time by the judge and jury. I going to ask you to come with me down to the jail. I'm placing you under arrest."

"Now, Marshal, I have never been arrested before."

"That's right, Marshal, my baby has never been arrested before" the girl stated.

I was watching as he removed the thong from the hammer of his Colt, while she was hugging him. I thought on what Mr. Tillman had said - he is a fixin' to drop the hat. I went ahead and stood up, then I fell for the oldest trick in the book. As he got to his feet he snatched the girl right in front of him and went for his pistol, leaving me with very little target to shoot at. She was much shorter than he, and his head was a perfect shot, but not before he got off a shot at me. I guess we fired at the same time.

It was much later that night when I woke up in Doctor Childer's office, with people standing all around. As I opened my eyes, Elizabeth was sitting in a chair at the head of the bed. She laid her hand on my arm.

"You like to have met your Waterloo, Marshal Blunt, I don't know what that feller shot you with, but it certainly made a hole," Doctor Childers said, as he bent over me checking my vital signs.

"What about the other feller, Doc?"

"You reduced the world's population by one outlaw!" the doctor exclaimed, taking a step back.

"You got e'm right between the eyes, Father," Billy said, standing at the foot of the bed, looking on.

"Billy Blunt!!!! You could have put it some other way," Elizabeth scolded.

"Marshal, I had to dig the chunk of lead out of you, and you might as well make it up in your mind, you are going to be bedridden for a few days, if me and Elizabeth have to hogtie you down"

"The way I feel right now, Doc, you won't have any argument out of me." The next few days I had lots of visitors, including Mr. Tillman from the Seed and Feed store.

"Marshal, I told you that feller was meaner than a snake."

"You sure did, and I just wasn't thinking clearly, and walked right into his bullet. You know we were just talking about that, not more than an hour before I got shot."

"Now, Marshal, if you need anything you just let me know. The whole town has been praying for you."

"I appreciate that Mr. Tillman; by the way how is the girlfriend, what was her name, Betty Lou Corbet, taking it?"

"I heard someone say in passing, she's glad he's dead...she was tired of him bossing her around all the time."

"I hate I missed Big Don's funeral, I did want to talk to his foreman, Mark Browder, about being my deputy." Mr. Tillman started laughing. "I know it ain't funny, but being your deputy is like being a lion-tamer; it has its drawbacks."

"You're right about that, they just don't last very long.

"What has the doctor said about your condition, are you healing up alright? Mr. Tillman asked, pushing his specks upon his nose.

"He said I might be able to ride in a few days, if I keep improving."

"You want me to talk to the other City Council members about Mark Browder? He sure would make a good deputy; he's a church going fellow, and all."

"Yes, I would be much obliged if you could tell him to stop by and see me."

"Now, Marshal, you take care of yourself, I have got to be running along."

Billy was coming into my room as Mr. Tillman was leaving. They spoke, then Billy came on in and took a chair near me. I could tell Billy had something on his mind. I could read him like a book, most of the time.

"Well?" I said.

"Well, we've got a problem! Maybe it's your problem more than mine and Mother's."

"Okay, now, say what you mean, don't beat around the bush, I am your father."

"It's what the doctor said this morning before he left."

"I don't remembering him saying anything."

"Well, Father, he didn't say it directly to you. Doctor Childers was talking to me and Mother in the kitchen, and you might have not heard him."

"Have you and your mother been talking behind my back? Shame on you two?!"

"No, no, Father, it's nothing like that; he was just telling us that you may not have full use of your gun hand for quite a spell."

"Son, I know that, I can draw and shoot with my left hand."

"Father, can I be honest with you?"

"Why, yes, my son, we're always supposed to be honest with each other, ain't we?"

"I guess so, but what I'm going to say is not easy, and Mother don't know about it."

I can say one thing, Billy had my curiosity running ninety to nothing.

"Father, I've been noticing here lately you have been getting slower an' slower with your fast draw."

My son's statement sort of took me by surprise.

"Maybe it's because you been getting faster and faster yourself."

"I don't think so, Father. Weren't you and Mother talking the other day about you having some arthritis in your hands? Didn't you say you had some pain and stiffness in your hands sometimes?"

"Well, yes, I did...but I didn't think it was slowing my fast draw down."

"Father, I'm going to talk to you as a friend, and not as your son...but I think you've answered your own question. Why are you lying in bed with a hole in your chest as big as your fist, when you had the drop on the man that shot you day before yesterday?"

"You don't understand, Son, he pulled the woman in front of him, then drew on me."

"Father, Father, don't lie there and make excuses to me, your son...you already said you saw him remove the thong from the hammer of his Colt. What were you expecting him to do, Father, just show you his pistol? You already knew he was meaner than a snake, according to Mr. Tillman. Go ahead, Father, and admit it, he out drew you."

I closed my eyes; I knew my son was hitting below the belt. "You're kinda rough on the old man when he's down, aren't you son?" I paused, but Billy stood his ground. "But it's the truth, everything you are saying is the truth," I admitted.

"Father, I said what I said in love, not to put you down."

"I know, I know, I should have realized my incapabilities before now. A man has to realize his limitations."

"Now you are talking like my father; but where do we go from here?" I had known this moment would come, but not this suddenly. At least I had someone to talk to about it.

"Father, have you thought what you are going to do when some one calls you out and wants to draw on you?"

"Not really, Son, I've been sweeping that scenario under the rug, up until now."

"Well, you and I can't 'put it on the back burner', as Mother would say, any longer."

I knew then my son was concerned about me. "Have you any idea what we can do, do I need to give up the Marshal's job, you think?"

"First of all, we need to keep this under wraps; if there is one gun happy cowboy within a hundred miles of Fort Worth, he'll come gunning for you."

"I say, don't even let your mother know what is going on."

"I say, you're right, but do you know what this means?"

I thought for a minute what my son was trying to say. "Not really, what are you talking about, Son?"

"I have to be standing in your shadow all the time."

"Do you know what you are really saying? Think about what you are saying; is this even going to work?"

Billy eased up and turned toward me. "It's got to work, Father, or...or..."

"Or what? Go ahead and say it; I know you mean well."

"I told you, Father, when I brought the subject up, it was going to be touchy. Look, Father! I'm not saying for one minute you are over the hill...or washed up as a U. S. Marshal... I'm just saying I love you, and you need some big-time help."

I listened to my son and grunted now and then, as he went on.

"I like the idea of you hiring Mack Browder, that is, if he will take the job...which I doubt."

"Why do you doubt he'll take the job?" I asked, cutting Billy off.

He pulled up a straight chair that someone that had brought in from the kitchen and sat down in it backwards facing me. "Father, I have ten good reasons on the tip of my tongue right now."

"Do any of them have anything to do with me getting shot again?"

Billy starting nodding his head, and took a firm grip on the chair. "Directly and indirectly they all do, Father, you can be a U.S. Marshal without kicking and clawing and getting shot. It's not your job to wallow in the muck and mire or to challenge small time hoodlums and drunks. For crying out loud, Father, the town of Fort Worth, Texas is large enough to hire good men to do those frivolous jobs."

I began to put some stock into what Billy was talking about. "You're saying hold the title of U.S. Marshal, but let someone else do my killing?"

I could tell this statement didn't set well with my son. Billy jumped up and turned the chair around. "No, Father! Do your work, work, work, if killing is involved, let someone else pull the trigger for a change."

"For God's sake, Son, you are talking about putting an old horse out to pasture."

Billy pranced around in the room for a minute or two. I just lay there waiting for an answer. I nearly laughed at what my son came up with. "At least the old horse didn't have a hole in his shoulder, big enough to see daylight through."

I have got to admit my sixteen year-old son had a point and made it well.

"Now, what are my two men in deep discussion about?" I looked up, and Billy turned around. There stood Elizabeth. "What is this about horses? I hope you two are not thinking about getting me a horse, at my age."

"Now, Mother, you have spoiled the whole surprise," Billy announced, starting to laugh out loud.

"You mean you don't want us to get you a horse when I get well?"

"No, I didn't want a horse before you got shot, William Blunt, and I sure enough don't want one now."

"Well if that don't beat all, Father, what else can we give Mother?"

Elizabeth came on into the room. "Are you two ready to eat lunch?" She picked up a few empty dishes and looked at me.

"Yes I am, I don't know about Billy, but let me get my clothes on; I'll be right to the table."

Now that stopped Mother in her tracks. "Billy run to the stable and bring me a rope to tie your father down, until he gets well."

"Mother, I believe you are serious this morning."

"You're dad-blame-tooting I am, and that isn't all I am, either."

"Listen, Billy at that language your Mother is using; I think she is serious."

I guess Elizabeth surprised both me and Billy as she turned and came back to the bed, fell on her knees, and burst out crying, I mean really crying, like I have never heard her. I was looking when she reached back and took Billy's hand, and pulled him down beside her.

"We nearly lost your father, Billy, did you know that...? Doctor Childers told me if the bullet had been a smidgen over to the left side I would have been a widowed woman, right now." Elizabeth started crying again. "I don't want to be a widowed woman."

Billy could tell his mother had completely lost it. He even felt so sorry for her, and knew now why she despised firearms. It took all he and I could do to get her calmed down and back to her normal self. She finally regained her composure and tried to get up, 'course I was of no help with my disability. Billy took hold of his mother and lifted her to her feet.

"I don't quite know what came over me just then."

"I do, Mother, you were just showing me and Father how much you love us," Billy answered.

"Yeah, that's right, Elizabeth dear...Billy is right, and we don't show it often times."

"Lunch is getting cold. Billy. William, I'll bring your vittles to you." I was well into my soup and homemade crackers, when I thought I heard someone knocking on the front door. The kitchen was a long way from the door. I guess Elizabeth and Billy were in conversation, and didn't pay any mind to the noise. I was sure of what I heard the second time; the knock was a little more pronounced.

"Just one minute, I'll be right there," I heard Billy yell from the kitchen. I listened closely but couldn't tell what they were saying. Then I heard Billy running up the hall toward my room. "Father, a Mister Peterson would like to see you; he said it will only take a moment of your time."

I quickly put on my thinking cap and tried to remember if I had had dealings with the man. "Show him in Billy, I'm through eating." I handed Billy my tray and he lit out for the front door.

I somewhat rolled around, making myself more comfortable, and waited for the visitor.

"The marshal is right in there, Sir," I heard Billy say, and a poor specimen of a man walked into my presence. To describe him would take too long, and I wanted to know what he wanted.

"Won't you have a seat, Mr. Peterson? You look like you are about tuckered out."

He sat down in the straight chair and crossed his legs, hanging his hat on his knee. He began to tell the saddest story I ever heard.

"Marshal, me and my wife came west a month or so back a ways. It was hard leaving Tennessee, with no money and two small girls. The wife and I were sharecropping for a farmer back there, south of Nashville. She and I weren't getting rich, by no means, but we had food on the table every meal that we sat down.

Now, Marshal, to make a long story short, my brother-in-law moved out here a little over two year ago and wrote his sister several times telling how good he and Gladys were doing; said he had started a little ranch just north of Fort Worth. Well, that just sit my wife and two girls on fire to come west and get rich.

Now, Marshal I got to admit, I was in favor of the idea myself. Sharecropping wasn't all that great, and as my wife put it - we would never own the land or the shotgun house we lived in.

You could say I'm right handy with my hands, and Grace and I bought a dilapidated covered wagon from some folks south of where we lived, and I started to work on it to come west. Grace and I bought the ragged thing for a song, and sung it ourselves. I don't believe there was anything on the broken down thing she and I didn't fix. It even had broken spokes in the wheels. We soon found out that oxen were more reasonable to buy, to pull our wagon, than mules and horses. She and I soon traded what little furniture we had saved up, and started buying one oxen at a time. Now, Marshal, training them to pull the wagon is a chore all of its own.

Now, Marshal, my Grace had worked her fingers to the bone sewing, canning, and packing to come west. Just one thing I haven't told you about, Marshal, the letters from her brother quit coming to us. Even though she continued to write to him several times, but no answers came.

'Course, now, Marshal, as in anything, you give the devil a place and he will take over. Grace and I began to wonder why did her brother stop writing to us? And naturally, she and I began to wonder...just maybe he didn't want us and our two squalling brats out there with him. Maybe I shouldn't have said that; Grace and I had two very disciplined little girls. We never thought at anytime something might have happened. Of course we never knew what was in store for us.

Chapter Twelve

The Marshal Listens To Wayne's Story

"How would you two gentlemen like to have a fresh cup of coffee?" Elizabeth interrupted, sticking her head in the bedroom door.

"That would be fine, Darling. What about you, Mr. Peterson?"

"I don't mind if I do, just black for me," he said, very gratefully. "Now, as I was saying, Marshal, the wife and youngins were turning cartwheels to come west, and I don't mind telling you, my feet were getting a little itchy myself. It had been over two months since we had heard from my brother-in-law, so we headed this way. Marshal, I don't mind telling you, I have made many a mistake in my lifetime but, Marshal… this was the biggest."

Elizabeth served our coffee and left the room.

"Now, Marshal, to say it was an easy trip from Nashville to Fort Worth, I would be lying; it was near impossible at times."

I watched as he took a sip of his coffee and wiped his mouth on his long sleeve. I had nothing more to do but listen to his story.

"Marshal… Grace and I lost our first daughter crossing Arkansas, with fever, my wife said… the second, the same way, a week later. We even thought about turning back several times...but turning back to what. As you can see I made it out here."

"That was some story, Mr. Peterson. Why did you come to see me? I'm sure you didn't come to tell me that story."

"Oh, no sir, Marshal, I just come to tell you when you come to arrest me, I will give you no trouble."

Now this statement I didn't rightly understand. "Why would I need to come and arrest you, Mr. Peterson?"

"For killing three men," he replied.

"Surely not, Mr. Peterson, maybe you need to tell me the rest of the story. Did you ever find your brother-in-law?"

He finished his coffee and set the cup on the nightstand beside my bed, then straightened back up and started his story again. "Maybe that would help; as soon as the wife and I made it to town we went by the land title office and asked where my brother-in-law had his land recorded. I might say they were very nice and told us exactly where he lived. At that time the wife and I hadn't eaten in several days, she and I had run out of everything. My wife and I had no trouble finding the property. There was even a small cabin he had wrote us about."

I couldn't wait to hear the rest of the story.

"Marshal, there was a few chickens scratching around in the front yard, and the front door was sprawled wide open. I helped my wife down out of the wagon and she and I moseyed inside. At first glance we could tell that there hadn't been anyone living here in weeks. There was a picture of my brother-in-law and his wife settin' on the mantlepiece, undisturbed. There was canned stuff in the pantry, but no sign of my brother-in-law nowhere to be found; we even looked out in the back yard for graves.

My wife found a bag of dried beans the rats hadn't carried off, and a cruse of oil, and a tin near full of flour. I fired up the wood stove while she was mixing up some biscuit dough. We just figured we'd have the beans for supper, along with some onions growing in my brother-in-law's garden. While the biscuits were baking, my wife and I began to put two and two together...it was for sure her brother didn't just up and move off with out notifying her. Although the house was ransacked, both Grace and I noticed most of his and his wife's personal belongings were still here.

While we were finishing up the hot biscuits and grape jelly, and washing it down with steaming black coffee, we heard horses ride up. 'Course the front door was still sprawled wide open. I quickly eased up and walked to the door, and looked out.

'Can I help you gentlemen?' I asked the three men on horse back. They looked at each other and rode over to our wagon.

'We saw your smoke; you folks just passing through?' one of the men asked, riding back up a little closer to the house.

'No sir, I can't say that we are, this is my brother-in-law's place and we're looking for him... we've came all the way from Tennessee.' The man whipped his horse around and rode back to where the other two sat. I listened but couldn't make out what they were saying; I just knew it wasn't good, by the expression on their faces. Soon the two started riding off and the spokesperson for the bunch rode back up within a few feet of me, and pulled his horse up.

'Mister, you better be gone by sundown! We're coming back, and if you are still here it will not be good for you or your wife.'

I noticed Grace had come to the door. The man never said another word, but rode off, catching up with the other two."

"Why don't you gentlemen finish the rest of this pot of coffee, so I can wash the pot and make some fresh." Elizabeth brought the pot this time and poured us two cups, then left the room.

"Now, Mr. Peterson, evidently the cowboys did come back as they said." I could tell Mr. Peterson was getting very uncomfortable with the rest of the story.

"Oh, yes, Marshal, they came back alright! The sun was going down and Grace was putting supper on the table; the beans was done and she had made some fritters. They began to shoot the place up, then rode back and forth killing the oxen and all the chickens in the front yard. I was standing at the front door trying to make a dash to the wagon to get my rifle and old pistol. Marshal, I thought the shooting would never stop. As soon as they rode off I ran to where Grace was lying, on the kitchen floor in a pool of blood." Mr. Peterson choked up and began to wipe his eyes on his sleeve.

I didn't know what to say, I had heard enough for one lifetime. "Mr. Peterson what did you do with your wife's body?" I asked. I watched as he had to relive the saddest moment of his life.

"Marshal, I picked up my loving Grace in my arms, and started down back of the cabin. As I walked past my brother-in-law's makeshift garden, there was a shovel sticking in the ground that I grabbed and carried with me". Marshal, I don't know how far I walked, but I walked until I collapsed. My heart was pounding so hard and fast I thought I would die, then I kept feeling my Grace's warm body, as it grew cold and stiff. I remember I laid her flat in the grass, and gently folded her arms - that would never again hold me on a cold winter night. I made sure her eyes were closed, and I started digging the grave. All the time I was digging, I remembered digging the graves for my two girls, along the way. It was nothing like this, Marshal, I knew I had a loving wife to console me when the burying was done with little daughters. I dug her grave so deep, I could barely climb out when I had finished. I took off my bandana and tied it over my wife's face...the thought of throwing dirt in my Grace's face was unbearable.

With blisters on both hands, and my tongue stuck to the roof of my mouth, I leaned back on the mound of dirt and went hard and fast asleep. I woke up the next morning, it was way on up in the day; the sun was bearing down. I started back to the cabin, which was a ways through the trees and brush. I thought it strange that I smelled smoke. As I approached the ashes of my wagon and where the cabin once stood, I knew the mob came back and finished the job."

"Mr. Peterson, it not right for any man living on God's green earth to have to go through what you went through. And I don't have the answer' but if you will wait until I get well' my son and I will go with you and arrest the men that are responsible for your wife's death."

"Marshal, this is all my doing, and I don't want to put you out; I have no life any more. Look at me... all I have on this earth is the dirty clothes on my back, and not a cent in my pocket. Marshal, I don't know where the next meal is coming from."

"Well, I do!" Elizabeth exclaimed, coming back into the room. "I hope you men will forgive me for eavesdropping, but I heard most everything you said, Mr. Peterson."

"Mr. Peterson, this is my wife Elizabeth, she is the preacher in the family."

"Yes... and I have a word for you, Sir, and it is straight from God." I didn't quite know how Mr. Peterson was going to respond to my wife, giving him a word from the Lord.

"The Lord is not through with you, yet, Mr. Peterson. What the devil meant for bad in your life, God is going to use mightily in His work, and He is going to start this very day. Do you have a first name? We're calling you Mister, and my husband and I are older than you."

"It's Wayne Presley, Mrs. Elizabeth."

"Well, good, Wayne, first of all the marshal has something he is dying to tell you, and it will be from the Lord."

I thought to myself, 'I do?' This was news to me.

"Go ahead, William, and start talking, the Lord will fill your mouth."

Poor old Wayne just sat there, looking back and forth at us.

"Wayne Presley, is it? You was telling me you were good with your hands," he nodded and I went on, "I want you to go with my son, Billy…He will take you down to Art's Dry Goods Store and buy you a complete changing of clothes: including hat, belt and boots. Billy, tell Art I will settle up as soon as I get out of bed. Now, Billy, you and Wayne go up to our gun shop, and you help him pick out a pistol and fast draw holster. Is that all clear?" Both Billy and Wayne looked at each other, then nodded. "Then you two go over to the jail, and you can pin a deputy star on Wayne's shirt. Do you have all that, Billy."

"Yes, Sir."

"Then you and Wayne go over to the hotel and get a room for him. Tell Smitty I'll settle up as soon as I get on my feet. Now, Wayne, you go get cleaned up and come on back over here, and Elizabeth will have dinner or supper, or whatever you call it, setting on the table."

"But Marshal......."

"Wayne, I don't want to hear any buts. I just hired you as my deputy, and you start right now. And I'll see you and Billy at the supper table in about two hours." I could tell that was right down Billy's alley. I heard the front door slam shut as they left.

Elizabeth retrieved the two coffee cups and look at me and smiled.

"Are you sure the Lord gave me all that to say darling".

"I guess so, you said it."

"But I wasn't going to say all that, Elizabeth, darling."

"Didn't you just get through telling Wayne there are no 'buts' in all of this? Let me go and start dinner before I start calling it supper."

As I lay there feeling sorry for myself, I remembered a poem I has read when I was a boy back in Ohio. I don't know just how it goes, but the author of the poem said: 'I felt sorry for myself because I had no shoes to wear, until I met a man who had no feet.' I guess I must have dozed off for a while, for the next voice I heard was Elizabeth's, calling me to sit up and eat dinner.

"The boys are back from town, William, and you wouldn't know Wayne, all clean shaven with new clothes on. William, the Lord used you today, don't you feel good inside?"

"Now that you mentioned it, Elizabeth, I guess I do. When they get through eating tell them I need to see them for just a minute." I was still eating when Wayne and my son came in my room and sat down.

"You wanted to see us, Sir?" my son asked, with Wayne looking on.

"Yes, I did. I might say, Wayne, you don't look half bad, all cleaned up and new clothes."

"I owe it all to you, Marshal, and your son sitting here."

"Well, let's give the Lord a little credit. But, I wanted to tell you, Wayne, that star you are wearing gives you the right to shoot someone legally, and not to get into trouble. You have already told me you were going to kill three men, and I would have to arrest you. The hand of the law is on your side now; but you always remember to uphold the law and order. Do you read?" I asked

Wayne quickly looked over at my son, Billy, and nodded.

"Yes, sir, I read good."

"In that case, my son has got some books that you need to read in your spare time. 'Course I never read 'em...but look where I am. You and Billy will start lessons on shooting and fast draw the first thing in the morning; that's an order. Are there any questions?"

Wayne looked over at Billy, then back at me and asked, "When will I avenge my wife's death?"

"You won't!" I could tell right then that I had some explaining to do. "Wayne, you listen to me, and you listen good, you let that deputy star you are wearing do the avenging for you from now on. A good lawman never inflicts harm for a wrong that has been done...you let the law work for you...and never forget you are the law, as long as you wear that badge."

"But, Marshal!"

"There are no buts in this, Wayne, it is the law. You will probably have to kill every one of the men that shot your wife...and as they fall to the ground you can say under your breath, 'Darling, that is for you'. Do you hear what I'm saying?"

Wayne seemed to understand, and his hate and hostility were smoothed over somewhat. "One other thing, this will be the last meal you will eat at this house, unless my wife, Elizabeth, gives you a special invite; you will eat at Joe's Café, unless you do a little baking on your own. All business will take place at the jail, not here at my home. You might say that Billy is your boss, until I get out of bed and get better."

We left it at that, and a week passed off quickly. Billy was giving me a progress report on Wayne, and how things were going on down at the jail, daily. Doctor Childers was giving me good reports, and Elizabeth was feeding me too much. Billy was telling me that Fort Worth was going 'to hell in a hand basket'... maybe not in that many words. As they say, 'when the cat's away the mice will play'.

He told me that the big saloon they had been building on for so long had opened up, since I had been bedridden. And I'm sure that didn't help matters in town one bit. It was that very evening Billy came home and told me that Old Man Foster had lost his ranch to the new owner of the Music Box Saloon. As you know, the curiosity that killed the cat got the best of me, and I had to ask what happened.

"As you know, Father, I don't go into saloons unless it's an emergency...but the best I can tell, and what I have heard second hand...Mr. Foster was in there playing poker, and the stakes were pretty high, according to Ben Robinson, who was sitting at the table when all this happened. It seemed that Old Man Foster had a right decent hand; when the betting started he said all the other men in the game threw in their hands, and left Old Man Foster and the new owner of the Music Box Saloon to finish the game.

He then said the owner raised Old Man Foster a thousand dollars, which he didn't have on him at the time...but gave his ranch as an IOU for the stakes in the game, to cover the bet. Then Ben Robinson said, while the transaction was going on, the waitress brought the new owner a drink, and as she neared the card table, she stumbled and fell on Old Man Foster. Ben said she wallowed all over Old Man Foster before she could get her footing. Well, to make a long story shorter than it is, it just so happened Old Man Foster didn't have the winning hand, and he lost his ranch."

"That's too bad, I knew his gambling was going to get him in trouble one of these days." I said, rolling over to get more comfortable.

"Father there is more to this story, it gets worse."

"Go ahead and let me have it, what could be worse than losing your ranch?" Billy looked a little taken in, when I said that.

"Ben Robinson said for certain, the old man knew his hand had been switched, and he was cheated. As it turned out, Old Man Foster got all worked up, and after a few drinks he went out to his horse to get his Henry, and was gonna show the new owner a thing or two. As it was, when he came staggering back in the saloon as he neared the poker table, holding his rifle, the new owner whipped out a Derringer and shot Old Man Foster two times, right through the heart."

"Well, I guess that's worse than losing your ranch. By the way, Billy, how is our student coming along with his pistol lessons? It's been a while since I asked."

Billy began to smile, I knew he had a good report.

"Now, Father, you ain't going to believe this...but Wayne took to that Colt peacemaker like a duck takes to a mud puddle. He is might near as fast as I am, 'course his accuracy stinks. But, as I told him, 'practice makes perfect'. I can tell you something else, Father, if you got time to listen."

"Now, Son, that is the understatement of the day; what else have I got to do but lay here and hope to get well?"

"Well, we all hope you're getting better by the day, but what I was going to say - I think Wayne is going to make a good deputy; he is very well educated in book learning, and he can out read me."

I thought back to what Elizabeth had said to me that day as I talked to Wayne; she said I had a word from the Lord. As far as I was concerned, as I looked at Wayne sitting there in old, dirty clothes, needing a shave - to me, he was just a bum with a sad story to tell. But, now, as I looked back and listened to Billy, I knew that God was looking on Wayne's heart, and not on his clothes.

I guess I had momentarily dozed off, because when I opened my eyes, Billy had left the room. I lay there thinking on all that Billy had said...how Old Man Foster was going to take the law into his own hands. I'll admit, the law around Fort Worth was not up to snuff, but it's the law and it was all we had.

I was waiting for Thursday to come. Doctor Childers had promised I could get up and walk around, and I'll be the first to admit, I'm not a bad person and I was glad to get up.

"What are you doing home this early, Son, are you gonna celebrate my getting up and walking out on the front porch?"

"No, that is not why I'm home, but I glad you are able to get up today. But, I think we have a problem...Wayne thinks that two of the men that shot his wife and burned his brother-in-law's cabin down, are over at the new saloon."

"Is he sure?" I quickly asked.

"I don't know, but he said he was over by the Music Box Saloon and they walked right by him, and they didn't even recognize'em, with his new clothes and being clean shaven. Now what do you think we ought to do?"

"Let me think this through for a minute: this is some big time stuff. These cowboys don't go to Sunday school, and they probably are not wanting to go to jail, either. Do you think Wayne is good enough with his pea-shooter, if either one of' em pull down on you and him?"

"If not, I can take up the slack, you know that Father."

"I know that, Son, but you are so young to be killin'."

"Look, I believe this is my calling, and if there was ever a bunch of no good buzzards that needs a good killing, it's them two. I heard Wayne's story, what they did to him."

"You know I'm not going to be there to help you and Wayne."

"I know, Father, but we can handle the job."

"Let me give you some good advice, Son, I didn't take for myself. You don't go into that saloon without a plan; you and Deputy Wayne give it some thought... have plan A and plan B, just in case things don't work out."

"Can I help you out to the front porch swing before I leave? I know Mother is over at the hardware store, working on the books, since it's Thursday."

"I don't mind if you do, I'm still a little weak."

I'll let Billy tell this part of the story. . .

I left Father sitting in the swing, looking out across the yard, waiting for Doctor Childers to come by.

I knew that Wayne was supposed to be waiting on me at the jail. Sure enough, he and Miller Davis were huddled up around the coffee pot, discussing the price of rice in China, when I walked in.

"Well, what did the marshal say?"

I could tell that Wayne was gung-ho, and chomping at the bits, to see that justice would be done to the two killers.

"He said you and I could arrest the two men, and put 'em in jail." I could tell that Wayne was somewhat surprised, at first.

"He did!"

I guess he knew that 'the dog had caught the wagon, and didn't know how to drive it'.

"You've never gone up against a man before, have you?" I asked getting me a cup.

"Well... not like you're talking about, and surely not men with pistols, that can shoot back."

"Are you scared to go up against them?" I asked, as I poured me a cup of coffee.

"Not really scared of them, but of myself and what I might do."

I walked back to the front of the room, to sit down.

"I'm glad you said that". Father said we needed a plan, " I said, as Wayne sat down across from me." "We walk over to the Music Box Saloon, making sure our Colts are fully loaded and the thongs are off the hammers. Then you and I swing the bat-wings open and step inside. We look all around until we spot the two men that we are going to arrest. what could be simpler?" I explained.

Wayne responded a bit edgily, "That is the easy part, Billy, keep on talking."

"As you and I look all around, we spot them; they are either standing at the bar, or sitting at a table; either way we have the upper hand. They don't know we're coming, or who we are. Make sure your Colt is loose in your holster as we start to approach them. Do you want to do the talking, or do you want me to talk?" Wayne was lost for words. "Okay I'll do the talking...but you cover my back and if they make a false move, you draw, and get ready to shoot. I know you're not the best shot in Fort Worth, but at close range you can't miss, do you think?"

Wayne, all of a sudden, didn't look so good. "Do you think there will be shooting?"

"Does it rain in Spain?" I asked, knowing full well there was going to be a killing before it was all over with. "Are you ready to go?" I then looked over at Miller who was finishing up his cup of coffee, "Do you want to go with us, Miller?" he nodded. "Then bring a pair of handcuffs with you, we might need 'em."

Chapter Thirteen

Billy Kills Two More Men

The three of us made our way on down to the new Music Box Saloon. Miller and Wayne were not saying much, and lagged behind. I stopped at the bat-wings, and they caught up. I peeped in and quickly looked all around. The seven or eight piece orchestra was going full blast, and a stage show was in progress. I really didn't know who I was looking for, so I reached and pulled Wayne up beside me.

"See if you see those two buzzards in here anyplace."

It seemed we weren't even noticed; all eyes were on the free stage show. There must have been a dozen or more beautiful girls dancing. About all the ladies were wearing were high heels on their feet, and smiles on their faces.

"There they sit, right up close to the edge of the stage, over on the left side."

"Are you sure that's them?" I asked, stepping inside the saloon.

"I'm positive, Billy, I swore I'd never forget them two faces, as long as I live."

"We might have to wait until the show is over. I can't even hear my self think, the band is so loud...can you, Wayne?"

"What did you say, Billy? The band is so loud I can't hear anything."

I motioned with my head for us to move on down closer to where the two polecats were sitting, nursing beers. Both men looked to be in their late thirties, and could probably hold their own in a butt kicking contest. I was hoping that Wayne wouldn't come unglued and start shooting. It was no telling what Wayne was thinking, about what this scum bag had done to his wife.

I stood there in the crowd of drunk cowboys. They had all moved down closer to the stage, to see the girls. You might say the situation was totally out of hand, and confusion had set in. Nothing was like we had planned. I looked over at Wayne, shrugged my shoulders, and twisted my mouth as if to say, 'what now?'. Both men were now standing up, to see over the crowd that had migrated down to the front. Believe it or not, there were even some inebriated cowboys standing on top of the tables. I was certainly seeing things I had never laid eyes on before, and having other experiences I would need to pray about later.

It was for sure this pandemonium couldn't go on all night. Two of the girls in the chorus line had fallen out on the floor; several cowboys had crawled up on the stage and were inching their way over to the girls, who were lying on the stage. I guess if it hadn't been for the two or three bouncers with ball bats there's no telling what might have happened. I was plumb embarrassed, and didn't even look over at Wayne or Miller. I remembered Father had said to have a plan, before we even went into the saloon; but plans A, B and C were all used up, and we certainly didn't want to change horses in the middle of the stream. It had even crossed my mind to ease up behind the men, and do my best to bend the barrel of my pistol over their no good heads, then drag them outside. I knew that Wayne would go along with that plan; but then I thought that might not be the wisest choice.

I motioned to Miller, and pulled on Wayne's shirt, to let them know to get out of this crowd, until things got back to normal. We were standing near the entrance of the saloon when the girls started running off the stage, behind the curtain. The orchestra began to simmer down to a low note, and the drunk cowboys began to jump off the tables. I could tell that plan A and B had failed when the two men didn't sit back down at the table. Instead, here they came, right straight for the exit. I made sure the thong was clear of the hammer of my Colt, and it was loose in my holster. Then I stepped in front of the bat wings, blocking the entrance.

"Hold it right there, Gentlemen! I need to have a word with you two."

They stopped dead in their tracks sizing me up and down, looking at the deputy star I was wearing. "Boy, I don't know what you are trying to prove, but you look too young to die." He looked at his buddy standing beside him, "Wingo, tell this boy who I am!"

"Kid, you are in Bud, the Bad Boy's way; and you just better get out of his way, before he gets mad."

"Well, let me tell you who I am. I'm Billy Blunt, the marshal's son, and if either of you touch the butts of your pistols, I will drop both of you right where you stand." I guess my name didn't mean much to them; they started backing up.

"Boy, me and Wingo is two of the fastest guns in Texas, and you can't take both of us on at the same time."

Before the echo of his words went silent, I had drawn, and pumped two bullets into each of their chests. Without even clearing leather, they hit the floor, with blood running from their mouths. It became deathly quiet in the place, and the crowd began to gather around.

"Miller, if you will, run up to Craig Watson's office, and tell him he's got some work down here to do."

Most of the party-going crowd in here knew the two buzzards, lying on the floor dead, and knew the boy who brought them down. I could hear whispers among the onlookers, 'This is the marshal's son, Billy Blunt... the one who exterminated the Parlay family in one killing. I can't say that I was proud of it, but I came out of the shadow of my father that night, and my reputation as a gunslinger traveled far and wide. I don't know if that was bad or good, but from what I have been told by the old timers, and what I had studied and read here lately, if one is a fast gun - you can expect enemies that want to see if they can outdraw you. From what I have read, it's not like they are mad at anyone, they are just defending their title and reputation as the fastest gun; and usually that means someone getting shot and killed. I was hoping to keep a low profile on this fast gun news, but our local newspaper man in town, ol' Willie Pope, made a headline in the paper every time I sneezed. I told him a dozen times he was going to get me killed if he kept advertising that Fort Worth had the fastest gun in the west - and only sixteen-years old.

I don't know how Father knew what went on at the Music Box Saloon even before I made it home. I guess he had his sources. He was sitting up in bed when I entered his bedroom.

"From what I heard, you did what you had to do, Son."

I pulled a chair up to his bed, sat down in it backwards, and leaned over facing him. "Father, of all the people that have an ax to grind, or a dog in the fight, I hope you will be the only one who can sympathize with me. I didn't want to kill those two men, but they left me no choice."

Father started shaking his head. "Son, you don't owe me any explanation, I knew you didn't do anything wrong."

"But I killed two more men, Father, that's makes six men I've killed, and I'm not but sixteen-years old...well, near about seventeen in a month or so." I could tell Father was concerned about me in his own special way.

"Are you having regrets or nightmares at night about what you have done? I know taking a life away from a person is not an easy thing to do, even for a grown man."

"But you do understand?" Billy asked.

"Have you seen your mother today, since the shooting?" Father questioned.

I stood up, moved the chair back, and walked to the door. "I didn't go by the hardware store where she was today. I'm sure she has drawn up her opinion of me already, sad to say. I believe that's her coming in now, Father."

"Where are all my men folks?" we heard Mother yell from the kitchen.

"We're back here in the bedroom!" I shouted back.

Then Mother came walking in as if nothing was wrong, or had happened. "I must ask, William...how was your time sitting out in the swing on the front porch?"

"Wonderful, wonderful! I enjoyed every minute of it, until Doctor Childers came by and put me back to bed. He said: 'Let's don't over do a good thing the first day up'. But I did great."

"And what about your day, Billy? I heard you and your new deputy had a run in with the devil, and two of his workers."

"Yes, Ma'am, we sure did, and ever since it happened I've been wanting to ask you a somewhat religious question. Do you mind?"

"Oh, no, but first run to the stable and unhitch the buggy and feed the horse, while I start dinner for tonight."

I kept thinking to myself, as I left the room to do my chores, 'just how was I going to ask Mother about something that is spelled out in the Bible... 'Thou shalt not kill'. Why, that's the seventh commandment in the Bible; and it as clear as the nose on my face. Well, anyway, I'm going to ask Mother'.

By the time I finished and washed up for supper, Mother was stirring up pancake batter, and had the big skillet on the front burner of our Southern Comfort wood stove. The rich smell of coffee was all over the house...why it even brought Father to the kitchen table. He heard Mother say she was going to fix something fast, since she was so late from working on the books. And she knew pancakes were one of Father's and my, favorites.

"You can go ahead and ask me the questions you have, Billy. I can talk and fry pancakes at the same time. I'm just not sure I'll have the right answer; since you have aged, it seems your questions get more complicated every day."

"I think I have asked this question before, but I'm still pondering on the answer. The Bible says: 'Thou shalt not kill'. Are there any loopholes as you know of?"

Mother didn't say anything, but took a plate of pancakes over to Father, who sat at the end of the table. "William, go ahead and say grace over the meal, and dig in while they are still hot."

Mother went back to the stove and started frying again. I thought for a minute she might not have heard me ask the question, or was just trying to come up with the right answer for me. I was waiting on my stack of pancakes and for Mother to answer the question. I think Father was also interested in my question. Mother kept right on frying and never said a word. I was sitting ready to dig in, with a fork in one hand and a knife in the other. Finally, Mother turned around holding a plate of pancakes a mile high, with pure cow butter running all down the sides. She set them right in front of me. Father slid the syrup pitcher within reach; and I was ready for a treat.

Mother began frying again without saying a word. I hadn't forgotten my question, but right now it was on the back burner, as they say.

"Who's ready for seconds?" Mother asked, turning from the wood stove, where there were still several pancakes on the burner.

"I'll have a few more," announced Father.

"Me too, Mother, they sure are good."

"Best I ever ate," said Father.

"Ah, it's just because you're hungry tonight." Mother fried several more for herself, and sat down at the table across from Father. I pushed the syrup close to Mother's plate and leaned back.

"I haven't forgot your question, Billy, if that's what you're thinking." I didn't say anything but picked up my coffee cup.

"'Thou shalt not kill' means thou shall not commit murder. In the Bible, a just war is okay, as long as the soldier, or the man that is wearing the badge of justice, is fighting against an evil force. An example is the war that broke out in Heaven, between the good angels and the bad ones. That's why the archangel, Michael, is the patron saint for the military. There is a difference between murder and fighting in a war, or keeping the peace in Fort Worth, Texas. The command is 'Thou shall not murder'. God is pretty smart. He knows whether you killed or murdered. If the soldier has received Jesus as His Savior, all his sins - past, present, and future - are forgiven. He goes to Heaven." Mother dabbed the corner of her mouth with her napkin, picked up her fork, and started eating. I just sat there for a second or two, and let that word of wisdom and knowledge soak into my spirit.

"That's good, Mother, that is very good, I just hope you're right. I would certainly hate to go to hell for killing scum-bums and outlaws."

It was almost funny, the way Mother smiled at me when she said, "You'll go to hell for not receiving Jesus Christ, not for killing scum-bums and outlaws."

Father still wasn't able to ride, so Wayne and I decided to go after the other man who had killed his wife and burned the cabin down. Father gave us his permission. 'Only be careful,' he requested. Wayne was waiting on me when I got to the jail - chomping at the bits, raring to go. I guess we knew what was in store for us this Friday the thirteenth. He and I would normally have gone fishing. We left Miller Davis cleaning and watching over the jail, as we rode off.

"You reckon you will recognize the other yahoo who was riding with the group that killed your wife?" I asked, as Wayne and I rode along.

"I'm not sure, but I think so."

"Well that's all that matters. We'll let the judge and jury decide that."

"Suppose he don't want to go with us to jail?" asked Wayne.

"Well now that's strictly up to him," I answered. Father had given us good clear directions to the Walter King ranch, and I guessed we had been riding the better part of two hours.

"Is that a line shack over there?" Wayne pointed and asked.

"I believe you're right, it's too small for living quarters, unless you're a hermit."

"Well, it has two horses tied up around back. What do you say let's ride over and see if one of them is our man; it would save us lots of time if it was." Wayne and I turned our horses off the beaten path and eased toward the shack. I presume they heard us coming, because they had walked outside and were standing out front when we rode up.

"You two men lost, or do you always trespass?"

"We're looking for a man. I'm Deputy Blunt, and this is Wayne Pittman, also a deputy from Fort Worth."

"I'll tell you one thing, Stranger; you are looking for trouble snooping around on this ranch."

That statement nearly got under my skin. "It's our job to snoop around and find murdering polecats that have broken the law, Mister."

One of the men looked at the other. "He must be talking about Baker."

"What's this about Baker?" I asked, riding up a little closer to the two men.

"Well we heard his two running partners got gunned down in the new Music Box Saloon last evening. Do you deputies know anything about that?" I looked over at Wayne.

"You think we should tell 'em, Wayne?" he smiled and nodded.

"I'm afraid I'm the guilty party."

"You wouldn't happen to be the U.S. Marshal's boy?"

"Well, yes, I am. What have you heard?"

"Young man, me and Roger hope you don't get mad with us. We heard you are a fortune telling gunslinger; you know when someone is gonna pull down on you."

"Yes, and we heard yo' ma has prayed a wall so high around you the devil and a team of mean unicorns can't get over it, or a bullet can't penetrate."

 I looked back over at Wayne and said, "You tell 'em."

"You're dad blame tootin', that's right...his poor ol' ma has to get up every morning and hold a .45 Colt on 'em while he shaves, to keep 'em from cutting his own throat. Ol' Billy, sitting there, carries a switchblade in his back pocket, and a Derringer in his boot, and if you ruffle his feathers he will stick his knife in you, and walk all way around you, letting your guts spill all over the ground; and if you are lucky enough to run, he will shoot you in the back. Maybe you could tell us where Bad Billy and I could find this Baker buzzard. Do you know?"

The men started talking at the same time, "Yes, sir, Mister, he's up at the ranch house talking to Mr. Walter King; they got something big planned for tonight."

"Well, maybe we can join the party. Thanks very much for the information." As we rode off the two men stood there, like two wooden Indians. As we neared the ranch house I turned to Wayne and asked, "Do you have a plan?"

"I don't know why you ask, they don't ever work."

"Well, at least we have a plan, when my father asks - if we both get shot." I said.

"I'm gonna be standing right behind you, and the bad man has got to shoot through that high wall before he hits me."

I started laughing. "I don't know who started that wall business, unless Mother told some of the ladies in town."

"Well, she did pray a hedge around you, didn't she?"

"Yes, she did, but I don't know yet if it will stop a slug or not. But I may get my chance to find out. Is that our man sitting on the front porch with Mr. Walter King?"

Wayne leaned up in the saddle and looked. "I don't know until we get a little closer."

Wayne and I rode right up to the hitching rail near the front gate, and tied our horses. I always heard that Mr. Walter King was a likeable old cuss, but was so crooked that when he died the undertaker was going to have to screw him into the ground.

"You gentlemen light, and come in." I slid out of the saddle first, and watched Wayne do the same. I opened the gate and started up the cobblestone walk. I looked back. Wayne was bringing up the rear. I stopped at the steps and Wayne stayed behind.

Both men were in full view, sitting on the porch, and killing them would be a cinch, if push came to shove.

"Now, just what is it I can do for you two deputies?"

"Well, Mr. King, we don't know the name of the man sitting here with you, but we know his face and the horse he's riding." I was watching Mr. King. He was cool as a cucumber, but the man in question changed his facial expression, and started to get up.

"May I ask why you are inquiring about Barney?" Mr. King asked.

"First of all, we have an eyewitness who says he and two others, burned down a log cabin, shot four oxen, and killed a man's wife, not more than a few miles from your ranch." I'm afraid that was the straw that broke the camels back.

"Mr. King, these men don't know what they are talking about."

"Oh, yes, we know what we are talking about, and you are under arrest; we will ask you to come with us peaceably." I believed he would have reached for his pistol, but that would have added further to his guilt.

"Go with them Barney. I'll have you out of jail by tomorrow."

I thought right then, this ol' sly fox has something up his sleeve we don't know about; this is going too easy. "I'm going to ask you to give Wayne your gun rigging and boot pistol; you won't be needing them. And besides, it won't give you the idea of shooting us in the back on the way to town."

The three of us mounted up and rode off, leaving Mr. King standing on the porch conjuring up his next wicked move. I guess we had ridden a few miles when I eased my horse close to Wayne. "I hope you got eyes in the back of your head," I said.

"It's not what is behind us I'm worried about, it's the ambush up ahead that we better watch out for. I'm afraid you don't know this road like I do." I thought Wayne must know something I didn't. "Have you noticed ever since we left ol' man King's ranch we have been riding in a curve to keep from going through the bad land?" That I had noticed, but didn't know why. "Just as sure as there is a cow in Texas, that ol' cuss has sent men to cut us off up ahead. They will probably make their play when we reach the rocks up ahead."

It was for sure we were sitting ducks for anyone with a rifle, up in the rocks; it would be like shooting fish in a barrel.

"You say you know this territory, just where do you think they will likely strike?" I asked Wayne, being somewhat curious.

"I would think around this big curve, we have to go through a boxed in area and we will have no place to run or hide." Our prisoner, Barney, wasn't saying much. He had a smirk on his face, and I suspected he was just biding his time until the shooting would start.

"Lets hold up here, Wayne, I don't suspect our bush-whackers have seen us yet. We'll take cover in that thicket over there." After we left the main road and hid our horses we dismounted.

"What is your plan, Billy?" Wayne asked, taking his canteen off his saddle.

"I don't really have a plan, but it's for sure I'm not going to ride out there and get shot off my horse, in the open."

"You know, we could make a run for it, and take our chances." I couldn't believe Wayne said that, but with that kind of mindset he wouldn't last long as a deputy. I didn't say anything. I thought 'I have been reading a right smart here lately - what would the professional gunmen do in a situation like this? First of all, our enemy has the upper hand on us and is in charge of the battle at hand. We must turn the tide'.

"Did you say something, Billy?" Wayne asked, thinking maybe I'd been out in the sun too long.

"Yes, we must turn the tide, we must take charge of them."

"And how do you intend on doing that?"

"You stay here and keep an eye on our prisoner, and I'm going to circle around behind our gunmen, waiting up ahead in the rocks."

I reached for and retrieved my trusty Winchester from my horse, and was on my way. I used every bit of the cover I could, I even crawled at times, staying very low. Soon it all paid off. There were two horses tied up at the bottom of the hill, where the rocks started. Now, all I had to do was sneak up behind them and take their rifles. I knew that was easier said than done, but I inched on up through the rocks, keeping a low profile.

There they were, like two buzzards waiting on an ol' cow to die. I must have gotten within twenty yard of the skunks, without them seeing me. I hid myself in the rocks and began to think what I was going to say. First, I thought, I would just shoot both of them in the back, and come on back down out of the rocks and tell Wayne I had shot a rattlesnake, but couldn't find any men.

Then my mother's words came through loud and clear; now here is the difference between killing and murder. If I shoot them, its murder, but if I ask them to throw down their guns and they don't, I'll have to kill 'em.

"If you two men turn around or breathe, this is where you will die. You are under arrest for attempting to murder me and Deputy Wayne." They did as they were told, knowing they had stepped in their mess-kit, and their goose was cooked.

"Now, throw down your guns, knives and boot pistols, and start toward your horses, real slow and easy. If you even sneeze I will shoot you down like a mangy dog."

When they reached the horses, I could tell they had heard of my reputation shooting a .45 Colt. "Now, lead your horses and head toward the road." They did as they were told, and the three of us reached the main road. "Is there anyone else with you two, hidden on up the road?" They looked at each other and said something under their breath. I just up and shot the hat off the head of the man standing closest to me. "Speak up, man, I didn't hear that."

"I said, no, Sir! There is no one else up ahead in the rocks."

"Well, I hope you are telling the truth, because the first shot I hear, you will be the first to hit the ground with a bullet in your head."

I guess Wayne had heard the shot. He peeped out of the brush to see what all the excitement was about. Now, when bad boy, Barney saw I had apprehended the two men who Walter King had sent to bushwhacked us, he didn't know what to say. I still had two pair of handcuffs in my saddle bag that I used to cuff the boys I found in the rocks.

We made it back to town just before dark, and jailed our three criminals, knowing full well that Walter King was going to break them out as soon as he heard what had happened.

"We did good today, Billy, don't you think? I imagine the marshal will be proud of us."

"At least we didn't have to kill anyone, but you and I better come up with a plan...or our work will be for naught."

"You really think ol' man Walter King will break his men out of jail?" Miller had put on a fresh pot of coffee, and I eased over to the little stove.

"He himself might not do it, but he'll send men... and that's even worse. We have done killed two of his men, you know, and it's for sure he don't want these three polecats to go to trial before a judge."

"You know, Billy, I've only been out west a short time, but I can see it's hard for these old timers to accept progress, and law and order."

"You're right, Wayne, but it's coming. You take men like Walter King - it will be the death of them, to give one inch."

"That's right, and we still ain't got a handle on what happened to my brother-in-law yet."

Miller was sitting over by the back wall about to go to sleep. "Miller!" I shouted, "Where could I lay my hands on some dynamite?"

"How much do you need, Mr. Billy?" he answered with a yawn.

"I guess eight or ten sticks, but I don't know that much about dynamite, do you?" I asked him.

"I sure do, it ain't something to be playing around with. I had a favorite uncle on my ma's side of the family, to get blown to smithereens with dynamite."

I guess I should have left well enough alone, but now me, going on seventeen – would I ever learn? "Say he got mangled up pretty bad?"

Miller looked at me like I was a complete idiot. "Bad, bad, did you say bad?...Mr. Billy, they didn't find enough of Uncle Homer to have a good funeral. if it hadn't been for his old straw hat and rubber boots they'd not had a funeral. They even threw his old black powder pistol in the wooden box and buried it. That old gun is what caused all the problem to begin with."

Here again the curiosity that killed all them cats got the best of me, and I had to ask, "What did the ol' gun have to do with your uncle getting blown to smithereens, and where did the dynamite come into the picture."

"Over there, where Uncle Homer and Aunt Gertrude lived, was a beautiful, little, clear stream that run right in front of their shack. Well, to make a long story short, the devilish beavers had in time dammed the creek up, and completely cut the water from running."

Wayne had gotten interested in the story, and took a seat, sipping his coffee.

"Now according to Vernon, that was Uncle Homer's oldest boy, he and the ol' yard dog was traipsing along behind his pa when the whole thing happened. He said his pa had got fed up with that bunch of pesky beavers and decided to blow the dam up, so the water would run down the creek-bed again. He said his pa had asked Mr. Gene Watson over at the general store, to pick him up a box of dynamite, the next time he was over in Houston buying supplies for the store."

Vernon said him and his pa got up early Saturday and eat a bite of breakfast, and while he went looking for the shovel, his pa went by the barn to get the dynamite. He said evidently his pa didn't want to carry the whole box, and filled up all his pockets, hoping it would be enough to sabotage the dam. He said his pa had a head start, before he found the shovel, and he tagged along behind with the yard dog. He told me it was just before they reached the dam his pa stopped and yelled back at him, 'Hold the dog, here's a big rattlesnake!' and he saw his pa pull out his ol' black powder pistol to shoot the snake and that's the last words he heard his pa speak."

"Then you are saying you don't have to have a fuse and a cap, and all that rigmarole, for a stick of dynamite to explode?" I asked, working up to my next question.

"On no! That is why it's so dangerous; if it gets a good lick or gets jarred suddenly, it will explode, and explode any dynamite that is close to it."

"That's perfect, Miller. What if a stick of dynamite was shot with a rifle, and a slug hit it at a distance?"

Miller started smiling. "It would explode, along with any dynamite within any distance close to it."

"That's perfect, Miller. How long will it take you to get me eight or ten sticks of dynamite?" I asked, getting me a pencil and piece of paper to draw on.

"I'll be right back with some dynamite," Miller said, setting his coffee cup down, and heading out the door of the jail.

"Now listen up, Wayne, here is my plan."

"I just figured you had something up your sleeve, Billy; as much as you read." Wayne said, coming around to see what I was drawing. "I think we will both agree that ol' Walter King is coming to get his men out of jail, and whatever he does, it will be illegal. So, whatever we do to combat him from taking his men is within the law...do you agree?"

"Well, I guess so, whatever you say, it's either us or them."

"Now, here is my plan, it's for sure that ol' man King will come riding up in front of the jail...You and I don't know when, or how many men he will have riding with him. Are you with me so far?" He nodded and moved somewhat closer to see my blue-print of my plan. "When Miller gets back with the dynamite, we are going to dig a shallow ditch out in front of the jail, about where the horses will be standing, when they ride up and stop. Then we will cut the sticks of dynamite into small pieces and lay them length ways in the shallow ditch, and carefully cover them up." I was drawing it all out on the paper as I explained.

"Now, at the end of our ditch, that will be covered up and swept down with the broom, to look as nothing is there, we'll put a half stick of dynamite in a can, and set it on top of the first piece of dynamite that we buried. Now, here is the plan. No one will notice a single can sitting out there on the ground. When all of Walter King's men come riding up to the hitching rail in front of the jail, I will go out on the porch and see what he wants. Of course, you and I both know what he is going to say...I will agree with him and tell him I will turn the men loose, then come back inside the jail and slam the door and hit the floor. You will be next door, hidden with a rifle. You will shoot the can with the half stick of dynamite in it. Now, according to Miller, there should be a domino effect; and lord knows what will happen. After the explosion, I will run back out onto the porch and shoot anyone that looks like they haven't had enough, and then you run out into the street with you're rifle blazing and do the same."

Chapter Fourteen

The Big Explosion

Wayne and I had a shovel and hoe rounded up by the time Miller returned with the dynamite. The plan was simple enough, and the three of us went to work. Miller thought it was a fine idea, but advised us not to use too much dynamite. After we had finished, Wayne and I went back into the cell part of the jail, to talk to the prisoners. We had the two ambush boys in a cell, and the hardened criminal in a cell by himself.

"What do you think ol' man Walter King is going to do when he finds you three are in jail?" They all just looked at each other and smiled. "Do you want the truth?" one of the men asked.

"Yes, or I wouldn't have asked!"

"Well, to be truthful with you two, you both are wasting your time, and endangering your very life. I haven't worked for ol' man King all that long, but he will get what he wants."

"How long have you worked for the King Ranch?" I asked the other fellow in the cell.

"About as long as Dennis. My name is Oscar Keaton, and we're both from South Texas."

"Was either of you working for ol' man King when he got rid of the young man and his wife from back east, a few months ago? That was my brother-in-law .Tom Hardy. " They looked back and forth at each other. "I'm talking about the young couple that built a log cabin in the valley, south of ol' man King's Ranch."

"That was before we started working for him, but we heard what happened. And your brother-in-law isn't the only one ol' man King had killed, or run off their land."

"You better shut your mouth, Dennis Martin, we're in enough trouble already," Oscar Keaton ordered.

"Before you two clam up, let me ask one more question; how many men do you all think ol' man King will come riding in here with tomorrow?"

Again they looked at each other. "Well, he knows the marshal is laid up in bed, and there's just one inexperienced deputy and a fourteen year old boy that ain't dry behind the ears... it will be a piece of cake for him to just waltz in here and let us out."

"There is gonna be some waltzing going on alright," I said, leaving the three in the back to sulk. Then I instructed Wayne, "You and Miller watch the jail tonight, and try to get you some sleep. I'm going on home and tell Father what we did today, and I will be back early in the morning."

"You think all that dynamite we got buried will be all right out in front of the jail tonight?"

I couldn't help but start laughing.

"Now what seems to be so funny?" Wayne asked.

"We need to pray we don't have one of those thunderstorms like we had the other night."

"Yeah, or a dog don't come by tonight and start digging."

"Well, just make sure you run it off, for Pete's sake, don't shoot at e'm." We both started laughing.

Although it was late when I got home, Father was waiting up, and Mother was worried to death about me.

"Where have you been all day, Son? You missed lunch, and I'm saving dinner for you on the stove."

"Well, I can certainly use it, but Mother you are taking on over me too much." Mother poured Father a cup of coffee and he took his place at the table. "Father, it's going to be hard for you to believe what went on today." I told him the whole story.

"You are right, Son, you do have a lawman calling on your life; don't you think so, Elizabeth?" Mother finished putting my supper on the table and gave me a hug from behind.

"Maybe so, but I still don't like guns, Son."

"Have you and Wayne given any consideration to what ol' man King is going to do when he finds out you have three of his men in jail?" Mother poured me another cup of coffee, then sat down at the table to hear what I was going to do about the whole thing.

I looked over at Father he was all but in tears. "Son, what have I put on you? You are to young to be plagued with this responsibility. Look at me! I'm a poor excuse for a U.S. Marshal, let alone a father to a young son. Your mother is right; it's a gun that has caused all this trouble."

I didn't know what to say. It was tearing my guts out, watching my own father actually shedding tears over me.

"It's all right, Father, I can handle it."

"Stop it, Billy! To hell with this town and everybody that lives her. I forbid you from going back to that damn jailhouse ever again."

I jumped up and ran around the table and grabbed my father, "It's alright, Father, it's alright, you are just upset and it is completely normal."

"No it's not! It's not right for my son to fight my battles."

"Listen to Billy, my dear, I know God has given him a plan for tomorrow."

"You stop it, too, Elizabeth! You leave God out of this. Billy will have no part of this murdering varmint, Walter King; when he and his cutthroats ride into town and break his men out of jail, I know he will kill everyone that gets in his way...and that includes our son, if he is at the jail when he rides up."

"No, no, Father! I do have a plan. I didn't know that God gave it to me at the time... until Mother mentioned it just then."

"No, son! God doesn't have a plan to stop bullets. Just look at me and the fix I'm in."

"No, William, dear, don't say that. The Bible says all things work together for good for them that love him. Maybe God is going to work through our son to stop the mangy ol' buzzard you and Billy are talking about."

"Stop it you all! There is nothing that will stop Walter King; there is no reasoning with him, he is set in his ways and he thinks he is right."

"But he is not right, that is why he can't win this battle. His days are up in this town, you just wait and see."

I didn't want to tell him about the dynamite; I was afraid he might stop me from going through with my plan - thinking it might be against the law, somehow.

"Listen to me, Son! You too, Elizabeth. Billy, you get up early in the morning and go down to the jail, and turn those three men loose. Then come on back home, and your Mother will have breakfast ready. This town will understand in time; they should understand that two men can't hold off Walter King and his army of gunslingers." Father was beginning to settle down, thinking he had come up with a solution to the problem at hand.

"I have never come against you in anything, me being only a sixteen year old boy, but if I do what you say, I might as well go by and get the mayor out of bed, and let him give them three polecats a key to the city."

It took a minute for that true statement to soak in. Father bit his bottom lip and turned his head. You could hear a pin drop.

Mother broke the silence when she shoved her chair back, went to the stove, and brought the coffee pot back to the table. Father looked up and caught her gaze.

"But, Elizabeth," Father said.

"There are no buts in this family, William, you said so yourself." She stated, as she freshened up Father's coffee.

I could tell my father was pretty well set in his way, so I let him go to bed thinking he had convinced me and Mother that I would go to the jail early in the morning, and release the three men that worked for ol' man Walter King.

The next morning I eased our of bed and carefully put on my clothes. I fastened my gun belt on my body. and tied my holster to my leg. As I neared the kitchen. I thought I smelled coffee brewing. I was right. There was Mother sitting at the kitchen table praying. I eased up behind her and put my arms around her neck.

"Are you praying for me, Mother?" I seemed to have startled her. It was like she was in some kind of a trance at the time.

"Let me get you a cup of coffee, Son, you have plenty of time; your father is still asleep. Billy, I perceived in my spirit that you are not going to turn the three men loose this morning" Mother set the cup of coffee on the table, then sat down, pulling her chair as close to me as possible.

"Do you disapprove?" I asked. Mother took me by the arm and began to squeeze. "Yes, I do disapprove, but what you are doing has to be done, for this town to grow without crime and violence."

I told Mother to keep praying for me, and I would let her know how things turned out, after a while.

When I arrived at the jail, Miller was fixing to go and get breakfast for everyone - said he was just a waiting on me to see what I wanted.

"You ready for a big day, Wayne? I asked, as he kept fooling and fumbling with his rifle, watching Miller leave the jail.

"Just be sure you don't miss that tin can full of dynamite when ol' Walter King comes riding up, with all his hired killers."

"I don't think that's possible, I just hope it works."

"Well if it don't, just don't get in my way and make me run over you as I run out the back door," I said, without cracking a smile.

"Billy, do you have any idea what is going to happen when the dynamite goes off under those horses?"

"No, I don't, but I would hate to be one of the horses."

"You know, it's almost a shame to lame or kill a good horse to get to Walter King and his cutthroats, he remarked.

"I know, but he leaves us no other choice. We would be fools to stand out there on Main Street and shoot it out with him."

We had all eaten a good hearty breakfast and were biding our time. The sun was up and making long shadows. Wayne was ready to run next door and hide with his rifle, and Miller was watching up and down the street for Walter King and his men.

"Don't forget what to do, now, Wayne, when old man King rides up and I go out on the porch to hear what he's got to say...course we know what he is going to say before he gets here."

"Yeah, 'You turn my men loose, or we gonna tear this town to pieces, and if you try to stop us we will shoot you down.'"

"Yeah, that's about what he will say - word for word! Then I will tell him I will come in and turn his men loose. Give me time to run inside the jail and lay down on the floor, before you shoot the can with the dynamite in it."

About that time Miller came running inside, as if he had seen a ghost.

"They are coming!" he said, all excited. "It looks like ol' King, and three men on each side of him, coming in on the south end of town."

"Well, I'll see y'all later," Wayne said, heading next door with his rifle.

I reached up on the wall and took down a rifle and handed it to Miller. "If this plan don't work, you shoot ol' man Walter King dead, because he will kill all of us."

Many things were going through my mind, so fast. I was actually hoping time would stand still. Miller Davis was in the back, peeping out the only window in the whole jail, holding a fully loaded rifle. Wayne was hidden next door, watching the can full of dynamite.

I stood just inside the jail door, waiting for ol' King and his bunch of gunslingers to show up. They was in no hurry as they rode up in front of the jail. There were three men on the left, and three men on the right side, of Walter King. Before he had a chance to say anything, I moved to the door and took a step out on the porch.

"I've been expecting you, Mr. King!" He looked somewhat surprised, taking off his hat, then wiping his forehead on a handkerchief he took from out of his coat pocket.

"I can say one thing, Mr. King, you have got guts to ride up here and face me; as fast as I am, I could draw and take you, and probably both men sitting beside you."

He actually laughed out loud. "From what I have heard, you have more sense than that; you know you can't take us all, and you are going back in the jail and let my three men out of their cells."

"That is exactly what I'm going to do, but let it be known that you are breaking the law, Mr. King." I turned and started back into the jail, then turned back. "They'll be right out." As I went through the door I grabbed a hold and slammed it as hard as I could, and hit the floor. My belly had no more than touched the floor, when I felt like I was in the first stage of a earthquake. The concussion from the explosion nearly blew the jail house door off the hinges. As I got up and ran out onto the porch, the top was hanging down and in the way.

From the side view, I saw Wayne come running toward the seven men lying on the ground. As Miller came running out on the porch, I yelled to him, "Help Wayne gather up all their pistols and rifles!"

When the dust and dirt settled, and the smoke cleared, there were two horses down, and three standing out in the street with broken legs. The rest were hightailing it, back the way they came.

Two of the men were lying face down, and the others were sitting down, right where their horses had dumped'em.

"Go and get the doctor, after you have gotten all their guns," I told Miller.

It was for certain that the explosion had awakened the town. Here came Mr. Tillman and Jessie Brooks, to see what the noise was all about.

"Help me get all these men inside the jail and locked up; I have sent for Doctor Childers!" I said, trying to evaluate the damage that had been done. Ol' man Walter King was my first priority, and as far as I could tell, he had a broken arm and leg, both on the same side. The two men that were lying face down were breathing...probably knocked out. Being disoriented and not knowing what had happened, none of them could hear a word we were saying As other shop owners came running up to the jail to see what had happened, we managed to get some help to get all the men into the jail. Doctor Childers had his hands full and was asking questions, the same as everyone else. Wayne, Miller and myself weren't saying a word as to what had happened.

Some of the women folks standing around were saying it was an act of God; He had brought judgment to ol' man Walter King, and all his outlaw workers. Big John, our local blacksmith shot several of the horses with broken legs, then cared for the rest down at the livery stable. I couldn't say things would get back to normal, with Walter King in jail. With all his underground connections, and his money, it was for sure he could hire the best of the crooked lawyers, from back east.

It just so happened Wayne and I had gathered enough evidence of wrongdoing and murder, to put ol' man King swinging from the end of a rope. But as Father said, proving it and getting a jury to believe it, were two different things. Father had improved so much that Doctor Childers was letting him come to the jail several hours each day.

Now, other than the usual rowdy cowboys and barroom brawls and local drunks, Wayne and I assumed we had Fort Worth, Texas under the thumb of law and order. We also had ten men in jail who had to be fed three squares a day. And we had to put up with their moaning and groaning, let alone their bitching, dang near twenty four hours a day. Miller Davis, our janitor and gofer, had threatened to quit several times. The mayor and the men on the City Council were being paid off by ol' man King, under the table.

"By the time the Circuit Judge gets here, if ol' man King walks scot free, it wouldn't surprise me one bit," I said aloud, to no one in particular

As I said, my father, the U. S. Marshal...one and the same, had been coming over to the jail a few hours each day, under Doctor Childers orders, of course. With Deputy Wayne, and yours-truly, helping, the marshal was interrogating the prisoners, one at a time, in closed quarters. And I might add, he was finding out some very valuable information. For starters, we found out that Wayne's brother-in-law was killed; and his wife was taken hostage and sold, to a rancher named Max Pierce, who had a ranch west of Fort Worth, in a little town called Oak Hill. The killer that took her hostage went by the name of Lesley Lingo. And as far as the prisoner we had questioned knew, she was still with him.

Now, I don't mind telling you, when Wayne heard that his sister-in-law might still be alive, and not more than a two or three day's ride away, he was ready to go. And to tell the truth, I was ready to go with him myself. I did convince Wayne to let's wait until the court trial for the men we were holding in jail, was over. He agreed, but it took some arm twisting.

After the Circuit Judge arrived, the trials for all ten men didn't last but three days. The evidence that the marshal had, and the testimony of the other prisoners, put the rope around Walter King's neck, as well as the necks of the other polecats that did some of the killing. Several of the others were charged with lesser crimes, and sentenced to the state prison. The state prison wagon was guarded heavily, as all the prisoners were loaded and carried off to the big-house. That was where the hanging would be done. We all breathed a sigh of relief, but our work was still in the balance. Deputy Wayne was still chomping at the bit to go northwest, to find his sister-in-law. I'll be the first to admit I couldn't blame him one bit. It would be a piece of cake to tackle this job, after dealing with Walter King, and his bunch of thieving polecats.

As you will find out soon enough, we had our hands full with the bunch in Oak Hill, and if we had known more before we had lit out, Wayne and I might have taken more help, or called in the Texas Rangers.

Chapter Fifteen

It Was Just Short Of A Vacation

I guess we both needed a good vacation, after all the court trials were over and the jail was cleared out. I made it all right with the marshal, then Wayne and I started making plans to leave.

You would think that we were going to California, to see the way Deputy Wayne was stocking the pack horse with grub.

"Make sure we have a coffee pot, and a skillet, and a side of salt meat." I said, looking all around.

"I done got it packed, I'm gonna carry plenty of ammunition, and a couple of extra rifles."

"Did we have any of that dynamite left over, we could carry?" We both started laughing as he and I listened to the hammers and saws in the distance, putting the porch back on the jail house. It was about midday when Wayne and I left the general store, heading northwest. As he and I neared the hardware store, it was like a voice spoke to me: 'Go in and let your mother pray for you and Wayne.' I was a little skittish at first, but when we were right in front of the hardware store, the horses just stopped right in the middle of Main Street.

"Come on, Wayne let's go in and say goodbye to Mother." Wayne was still sitting there wondering why his horse had suddenly stopped in the middle of the street. He slid out of the saddle and followed me inside.

"I was waiting on you two," Mother said. I guess Wayne was wondering what Mother was going to do with the Bible in one hand, and a bottle of oil in the other.

"Lay your right hand on the Bible...both of you!" I obeyed, and Wayne followed suit and did the same.

"Father God, in the name of your Son, Jesus Christ, keep that hedge high and strong around my son, and You build one around Deputy Wayne that no devil in hell can climb over...Amen." Mother lay the Bible down and slowly pulled the cork from the small bottle of olive oil. With her finger, Mother dabbed a small amount of oil on the forehead of Wayne, then me. I caught Wayne's gaze; he was standing there with his mouth wide open - as if the cat had eaten his last cookie. Mother gave us both a hug. "God's speed to you both." She then turned an' walked to the back of the store.

Wayne never said a word as he and I mounted up and started riding. When we did talk it was about what were going to do when we found his sister-in-law.

"You don't reckon she has fell in love with this so-called rancher, do you, Billy?"

"Now, Wayne, you are talking to the wrong man about love affairs, I'm nearly seventeen an' never been in love."

"I see how that lil ol girl over at Joe's Café looks at you."

I didn't say anything, but wondered if other folks noticed things like that. "Well...looks is as far as it has got!"

"Now, Billy, I didn't mean anything about what I said."

"I know you didn't, let's just change the subject, an' let's camp beside this clear stream for the night. I tell you what... while you're trying to find that skillet and some hog lard' I'm going to see what's in that big black hole over there in that cypress an' juniper grove."

"You think we might have fish for supper tonight?" Wayne asked, dismounting.

"You get a fire going and I will guarantee it." I dismounted and opened up my saddle bag, and took out a hook, line, and sinker, and walked down to the big black hole, and looked at it. I took out my pocket knife, then cut me a nice skinny sapling about seven feet long. I stripped the leaves and few limbs from the sapling. Wayne was gathering up some firewood. I guess he thought I was serious about fish for supper.

"You want these two crickets that just ran out from under this pine knot?" Wayne asked. I finished tying my line on the end of the slim pole and rushed over to where Wayne was picking up wood. I caught both crickets and put one on my hook, made my way back to the black hole and gave the cricket a toss out into the middle of the black water. Wayne had become interested in my venture, and was practically looking over my shoulder. The cricket never stopped, one splash an' he was gone; something nearly jerked the pole out of my hands. Well, what can I say, it was nip and tuck as I played with whatever it was that wanted my cricket. Wayne was more excited now than I was. I was just hoping the hook wouldn't straighten out, or my line wouldn't break. Finally he, it, or whatever, got tired and came to the top, and I ran backward and pulled him, or her, right out on the bank.

"That's a green trout, Billy!" Wayne yelled, all excited, "I'll bet she'll go five pounds or more."

"You reckon so?" I handed the pole and the other cricket to Wayne. "You better catch yourself some supper, Wayne," I said, taking the hook out of the fish's top lip. I started back to the horses, where we had set up camp for the night, when I heard Wayne yell out, "I got 'em, Billy! I believe she's bigger than yours!"

Well, thank goodness he and I weren't fishing a rodeo; I would have lost for sure.

"I know what we're gonna have for breakfast in the morning," Wayne stated, bringing his big trout down to where I was in the scaling operation, "If you want to do the gutting and carving, I'll get the grease rolling, and mix us some hoe-cake batter...I wondered why I brought that sack of onions along."

"Wayne, I ain't much of a cook, Mother does all that around the house...if you will do the frying, I will unsaddle the horses an' string them out over there in that green grass."

Wayne agreed, and soon we were sitting around a campfire, getting ready to eat in style. We were about half through with our meal when a covered wagon, pulled by four horses, appeared in the distance. It was coming the opposite way from which we were heading.

I poured us another round of black coffee, and set the pot back close to the fire. As the wagon grew nearer, we could see there were two women sitting on the seat of the wagon.

"Woooo, up there, Maud!" the lady yelled out, popping the reins. Of course, the team of horses, being tired and needing a drink of water, had no trouble obeying the command.

"Is this the road to Fort Worth?" the youngest woman asked.

"It sure is, that is where we just left from, about noon."

"We could smell your campfire a mile or more down the road." The two women looked back and forth at each other as if to say 'we may need to stop here'.

"You ladies had supper yet?" Wayne asked, leaning back and rubbing his belly.

"No Sir, but we don't want to impose."

"Impose, my foot! We got enough vittles here to feed an army."

"That's right, ladies, we got more left than we can eat," I said, getting up and walking over to the wagon.

"We haven't eaten all day. My name is Daisy, and this is my big sister, Doris." I extended my arms, an' she caught hold, and I lifted her down from the wagon. Big sister climbed down from the other side, an' came around the back of the wagon.

"That coffee sure smells good," Doris added, approaching the campfire.

"You ladies help yourself, if you don't mind drinking after Wayne an' me, he only brought two tin cups." I could tell these ladies hadn't eaten in days. I had never seen anyone enjoy a meal as much as these ladies did.

"You know I believe I could eat fish three times a day I like them so well," said Daisy.

"I believe I could, too," Doris added, reaching for the last fillet of fried trout.

"I thought we would have fish for breakfast in the morning if you ladies don't mind camping here with us tonight."

"Now, as we said, Daisy and I don't want to impose upon you gentlemen, but we would feel much safer."

"We do need to unhitch your team and let them drink, then stake them out over in that high, green grass for the night." Wayne volunteered.

By the time our chores were finished - I punched up the fire an' put on another pot of coffee - it had gotten dark as pitch, and there was thunder and lightning back in the south west. As we sat around the campfire and got acquainted with each other, the weather seemed to have moved closer. The wind had picked up, an' one could smell the rain in the air.

"If the bottom falls out, we can run an' jump in our covered wagon an' close the flaps, to keep from gettin' soaking wet."

"I do appreciate the offer, ladies, but I brought some canvas to cover our foodstuff; I'll sleep under your wagon," Wayne replied.

I had an idea why Wayne had denied the offer of sleeping in the wagon with two strange women; his wife hadn't been dead all that long, and he was still in mourning, in his own spirit.

"Well, suit yourself, we tried; but we are going to keep Billy high and dry when it starts to rain," Daisy said.

"You mentioned you were going to Fort Worth. Do you ladies have friends there, by chance? Wayne or I may know them."

"No, I'm afraid not, we have never been there before, my sister and I heard the town was growing by leaps and bounds, and that we could get a job that pays well."

"What type of work are you two looking for?"

The two ladies quickly looked at each other. We heard a new saloon, called the Music Box, was hiring girls, and Daisy and I thought we would apply."

"Do you and your sister dance?"

Again they looked at each other. "No, we're afraid not."

"Well, you don't look like scrub ladies to me," I said.

"We're whores," Daisy said, turning her head.

I looked over at Wayne. He acted as if he wasn't surprised. I thought it awful to be young and dumb; 'course he was much older than me, and had been around.

"Well, I'm sure you women can find work; if not there, Fort Worth has five other saloons now."

I decided to change the subject. "Wayne and I didn't tell you that we are deputies in Fort Worth."

Daisy was sitting close to me; she reached over and pulled my vest open. "I don't see a badge!"

"We don't wear it when we're out of town. Every gun happy cowboy loves to use a badge for target practice." I reached into my pocket, pulled out my star, and showed it to the ladies. Suddenly the wind picked up and we could hear the rain coming. We all jumped up and ran for the wagon. The ladies had me by both arms, leaving ol' Wayne to fend for himself.

The ladies and I quickly jumped into the back of the wagon, and they did what was necessary to keep the water from blowing in where we were. Soon we were 'snug as a bug in a rug.' Doris lit a candle and started getting ready for bed. I didn't say anything, but watched the ladies pull off their long dresses and button-up high heels. It seemed not to matter to the ladies, removing their clothes in front of men. They didn't know I was getting an education, and an eyeful, at the same time.

"You want me to help you with your boots, Billy, I don't mind."

And before I could say yes, or no, both boots were coming off... Daisy had one foot and Doris had the other.

"You might as well take off your gun rigging too, Mr. Billy, I doubt you see anything in here to shoot tonight."

"I tell you what, Billy, I find you can sleep much better if you take those tight Levis off...here we can help you," Daisy said, practically getting on top of me; I was already laying down in the bed.

"Look, it's no use getting your shirt no more rumpled up than it is... let me hang it up until morning," Doris said, beginning to unsnap my shirt buttons.

"Billy, dear. Since you are our guest, we are going to let you sleep in the middle of the bed," said Daisy.

"Yes, it's much softer," Doris added. She lay on one side of me, and Daisy on the other.

I thought I would improve my education. "Do you ladies make pretty good money doing what you do?"

"Oh yes, and our repeat business is better once our clients get to know us." Daisy eased up and put her lips very close to my ear, "But you are going to get a free one tonight, Billy."

"I have never had one before, Daisy."

"Did you hear that, Doris? Billy has never had one before. I think we both ought to give him a free one tonight, what do you think?"

'I can tell you what I think', I thought to myself, without saying anything to the ladies: if Mother ever finds out I spent the night between two whores, she will disown me as her son.

"You want me to go first, Doris? I'm the youngest."

"I think that ought to be up to Billy."

"Do y'all mind if we wait a few minutes, until I can make up my mind?" I had never had a lady rubbing her fingers through my hair, or strange hands touching me. Did that hedge Mother prayed around me ward off devils only? I knew it was getting might weak; the ladies' hot breath on my neck, and the aroma of perfume was overpowering. I've heard it said that God is not always on time, but He is never late.

"What was that?" Daisy asked.

"What was what?" asked Doris.

"There it went again; someone is tapping on our wagon." Doris quickly opened the back curtain enough to peep out.

"Tell Billy we are going to have to move camp to higher ground; we are camped to close to the creek an' the water is rising fast."

It was still raining cats an' dogs. I quickly put my clothes back on and stepped out on the ground. I could see what Wayne was talking about. By the time Wayne and I got the ladies' wagon moved to higher ground, an' the horses moved an' settled down, it was dang near daylight; and it had put a damper on the 'free ones'.

By daylight the rain had tapered off. Wayne and I had sat under a tarp until morning. When the sun was high in the sky, the weather had completely moved out, thank goodness! And, thank goodness for the ax that Wayne had brought along on our trusty pack horse. Picking up dry mesquite limbs and twigs to build a fire, was out of the question; they were drenched. Chopping into a log lying nearby, Wayne discovered dry, rich wood, and a fire was soon started. The most needed coffee pot was on, to satisfy our morning addiction, Food would come later.

Not only were the horses chomping the green grass on the new stakeout, but Wayne and I spied a passel of large rabbits filling their hunger this morning,. I guess the several shots Wayne an' I made, directing our lead in the direction of the morning breakfast menu, had awakened the ladies in the covered wagon.

"I think four rabbits will be enough," I said, walking back to the campfire.

"I shore had my heart set on green trout this morning, but that's out of the question; our small stream has turned into a raging river," Wayne muttered, removing the rabbit meat from his hide.

"Daisy, dear, I believe this is the best rabbit I have ever tasted, don't you?" Doris exclaimed, stripping the tender meat from a back quarter.

"I shore do, Doris, the best I ever tasted, and these biscuits are just divine."

I thought to myself, sitting there watching the two ladies stuff their faces with both hands, have I missed something? I guess not I thought, I have no guilt to haunt me the rest of my life. Everything that is free is not free. I read that somewhere.

"You ladies should make it to Fort Worth by mid evening, if you will keep up a steady pace," Wayne said, reaching for our reliable blue granite coffee pot.

"Y'all did say you were coming back to Fort Worth when you finished your business in Glendale?"

"Oh yes, by all means, Billy's father is the U.S. Marshal there in town."

I was almost embarrassed by the next statement.

"Well, when you gentlemen get back in town, look us up. Doris and I will never forget who our friends are."

"That's right, when we met you fellows last night, Daisy and I had no friends, food, or money. And she and I hadn't eaten in days."

As we hitched up their team and got the wagon ready to travel I asked, "Would it be out of the question to ask why you two beautiful ladies don't go back home to family?"

The ladies looked at each other and hung their heads. "We were hoping no one would ever ask...but...considering you are friends, now, Doris and I grew up in a home with a very sickly mother. Both of us promised Mama we would stay and wait on her, until she got better, or died. Well, she never got any better, but grew worse daily. She hung on for nearly ten years, with us girls waiting on her hand and foot," Doris said, with tears in her eyes.

"Don't hate us for this, but Doris and I began to pray that Mother would die and go on to heaven so we could get away from our daddy." Tears came to Daisy's eyes as she told the story. "Our own daddy made us like we are; we had to satisfy his perverted sexual desires every night that rolled around."

"Yes, as long as I can remember, an' as little as I was, at times I grew to love it, God help me!"

"The same here, but Mother lingered on an' on, and just refused to die. Oh, our daddy provided for us well; he bought medicine an' had the doctor out to our ranch many times, to help Mama."

"Did your mother know what was going on between you girls and your daddy?" Wayne asked.

Again the ladies looked at each other. "Sir, she had to know! That is what made it so bad; she could hear us in Daddy's bedroom every night, laughing and cavorting, and dancing nude for our daddy."

"For the last four or five years, Daddy never darkened Mama's room door. He was afraid she would have a pistol under the cover, and shoot him dead. Mama was completely paralyzed, and could only move her eyes, when she died last month."

"What happened to your daddy after the funeral?" I asked.

"Well, Daddy stayed in town to drink and celebrate with the upper crust. Daisy and I came on back home, and took what money we could find laying around, an' saddled a good horse, and lit out."

"That's right, we knew we was pushing the horses too hard, but as luck would have it, we met a man with ten or twelve good looking horses on the road the next morning. We asked if he would swap us two fresh horses for our tired mounts. He could see we were riding good stock. He looked at Doris and winked, and after her and the cowboy came back out of the woods, she and I rode off on two fresh horses."

"Did you young ladies ever think about poisoning your daddy, or just blowing the s.o.b.'s damn head off?" Wayne asked.

"Oh yes! But we are whores, not murderers," Daisy explained.

"How did you ladies end up with a covered wagon?"

"Now let me tell you, the first night Doris and me slept on the hard ground, an' had to keep running off the wild animals. We knew this wasn't our cup of tea."

"That's right, we weren't going back, or going on, without something between us and the ground. Now this thought hadn't even left our heads, an' I guess we both looked at the same time. There was this covered wagon setting at this farm house, as plain as the nose on my face. Well, we just turned off the main road and rode up to the farm house. I guess twelve or fourteen dogs came running out from under the house. For crying out loud, you couldn't even hear yourself think. Well, finally, a man came walking around the house, toting a stick about six feet long, and went to beating and kicking dogs. I started one time to dismount an' help 'em. If there is one thing I can't stand, it is a barking dog; I don't have a nerve for that. Well, anyway, Daisy and I inquired about the wagon, and if it could be purchased. We explained that my sister and I was in dire need."

'You may have come to the right place.' he answered, taking a swing at the last barking dog. 'It belongs to my sister-in-law who just arrived from back east.' By that time, two women, that favored, walked out on the front porch. The farmer slightly turned and addressed the women, 'Adela, the ladies is inquiring about your wagon.' One of the women took a step forwards.

'What would you like to know?' she asked, bracing herself by holding to the porch post.

'Is it for sale?' Doris asked, volunteering to be our spokesperson in this wagon transaction.

'As I know' I have no further use of it... unless Josh wants to use it around the farm.' The man spoke up and walked toward the wagon. 'No, Adela, I have two wagons already, you might as well get shed of it while you have the chance.'

'Well, since the wagon was given to me, but I had to buy the team, you girls can have the whole kit an' caboodle for a hundred dollars.' Knowing very little about wagons, and less about horses, Daisy and I thought it was a bargain, and gave the lady our hundred dollars.

Then the man asked, 'What'cha gonna do with the two horses you ladies are riding?'

'Do you want to buy them?' Doris asked, as the farmer was explaining how we should harness up the horses to the wagon.

'Well, I'll tell you what, I'll I give you twenty-five dollars, an' throw in two sacks of grain for the saddles. That will probably be enough to get you where you're going.'

So here we are, ready to make it on to Fort Worth. Don't forget to come by an' look us up when you an' Billy get back home."

Wayne an' I stood and watched the wagon carrying the girls go out of sight; an' in our wildest dreams, we never had an' idea that Doris and Daisy would ever make it to town alive. We were both packed up and ready to ride; it was still early. With the sun to our backs, we were making good time.

"What do you plan to do when you find your sister-in-law, or have you gave it much thought?"

Wayne sort of twisted around in the saddle. I knew he had something to say. "I might ought to let this sleeping dog lay, but I fell in love with my sister-in-law, long before I married Grace...her younger sister."

"Are you thinking maybe you can pick up where you left off with Gladys? Your wife and her husband are no longer around, you know." I could tell Wayne was pondering that around in his mind.

"Yes I know! But is it right for me and her?"

"Well, I can't speak for her, but the Bible says man should not live alone, an' I guess you fit in there somewhere."

"You know, Billy, if Jesus thought it was such a good idea, why didn't he ever get married?"

"Wayne, ol' Buddy I have never wondered on that question, that would be a good one for Mother."

"Billy, I been meaning to ask you about your mother. Talk around town seems to think your mother is a fortune teller."

"I will admit she is strange at times, but I would call it spiritual discernment."

"I don't know the difference, Billy, isn't that kinda like a witch?"

"Oh no! Wayne, a witch is from the devil. Mother gets all her stuff from the Lord...the Bible says He only gives good gifts."

We rode on a little farther an' Wayne squared around in the saddle again.

"I hate to say it, Billy, but I don't know which witch is which."

I thought I was going to fall out of the saddle. "Wayne that is the funniest thing I ever heard."

"Well, when you get through laughing, you might need to help me think what we gonna have for dinner."

"You mean lunch, don't you?"

"Lunch, dinner, supper, snack, what's the difference? My gut tells me I'm starving; riding always makes me hungry."

"Man... them fish sure was good yesterday."

"You can say that again, I wouldn't mind re-licking that calf soon enough."

"We may get our chance. Isn't that a swamp up ahead? An' if it holds water, it holds fish."

"You got that right, an' look over there...a lightning struck pine, and the bark is just started slipping. We can get all the wood sawyers we want, for bait."

While Wayne was picking us off some bait, I rigged us two make-shift fishing poles, and you might say, he and I were in business. Now, if we could get some fish to cooperate with us, we'd be walking in high cotton.

Chapter Sixteen

Company For Supper

Wayne caught the first and second bream, they were good hand-sized red breasts.

"Billy, you must not be holding your mouth right," Wayne said jokingly, pulling another big bream out of the stream.

"I got one, Wayne! Look! Look! I believe he's gonna be bigger than yours, aw shoot, he got off," I said dryly, throwing the pole on the ground in disgust. "You go ahead an' catch dinner while I rustle up some wood an' get the fire going."

I walked off with an attitude and started picking up an arm load of dry mesquite limbs. Wayne found a flat rock in the edge of the stream an' went ahead an' scaled, then gutted, about fourteen nice size bream.

"Now, if don't have visitors today, we will have fish left for supper."

Well, the horses got a good break, and so did we. Soon we were on our way to find Wayne's sister-in-law.

"Wayne, I forgot where we are going. How will we know when we get there?"

Wayne pulled off his hat and scratched his head. "That's a good question, but the man said we would see a sign that reads - OAK HILL-1 MILE - right on the side of the road, as plain as day. And he also said it was a two or three days ride."

"Well, we still got a ways to go; I just hope we're not wasting our time," I said.

"I just hope we can find that cutthroat outlaw that did the killing, before we start back home."

"What was his name? I done forgot."

"Thank goodness, I wrote it down, now... if I can find the piece of paper... here it is. The rancher's name is Max Pierce, an' the killer's name is Lesley Lingo. You know there were three of them, as I told you, we got two of them, and this one left the country. I was thinking he might live in Oak Hill," Wayne said, looking over my way.

"Well, we're not on any strict schedule, or no certain time to be back home...I just believe you and I can track this buzzard down and get him hung."

"We might need to go through the court system first, don't you think?"

"I guess so...then hang em."

After several days of riding we spotted a sign up ahead, and when we pulled up we saw it read: OAK HILL 1 Mile. Wayne and I paused for a minute or two.

"Well, we made it, thank God. As my father would say: the dog has caught the wagon, but can he drive it?"

While we were sitting there, we saw a man on horseback coming our way. Wayne and I just sat there until he rode up.

"Good day, Gentlemen, y'all coming or a goin'?" asked the rider, looking us over real good, "We don't get many strangers."

"Is that a fact? I guess you might say, we're a comin'."

"Well... I wouldn't stay too long if I didn't have business in Oak Hill. They don't cotton to dead beats and troublemakers."

"I assure you, we're neither," said Wayne.

"It's hard to tell now days." The fellow kept sitting there. "You never told me what y'all are doing in Oak Hill."

"You never just came right out and asked us... and furthermore, we didn't think it was none of your damn business," Wayne answered.

"Now it's no use to get hostile, Sir, I was just going to do you a favor."

"The only favor you may do for us is point us in the direction of the Max Pierce ranch," I stated, getting ready to go on up the road.

"Well, why don't you and the young fellow settin' there just go ahead an take out your Colts and shoot each other...you will save Max Pierce the trouble."

And before Billy or me could say a word, the stranger kicked his horse in the ribs, and was gone.

"Hey!" I yelled at the top of my voice, hoping the stranger could hear me, "you never did tell us where Max Pierce lived."

The man didn't stop, but turned in his saddle and yelled back at us. "Next house on the left, two miles!"

"I wonder what that was all about...we should shoot each other; I guess he'd been out in the sun too long."

"You reckon Oak Hill has a café where we might eat a home cooked meal for a change?"

"Your guess is as good as mine."

And we kept on riding. I think we had gone the better part of two miles when we came to a fence with a big iron gate.

"It looks like Max Pierce is serious about folks trespassing on his land." A big sign read: Absolutely No Trespassing - Intruders will be shot on sight. "Well, I can say one thing, that's about as plain as it gets, I ain't hankering to get shot no time soon. Are you?"

"Let's ride on up this road and see if there is an eating joint of some sort."

We hadn't ridden but a short ways; I guess a mile and a smidgen, when we saw a few buildings that some ways resembled a small town. As Wayne and I drew closer, we were surprised to see another sign that read: Oak Hill Dead End. You might say everything looked normal to us at first glance. We rode by the livery stable and blacksmith shop and were nearing Pierce's General Store, when Wayne and I noticed that Main Street ended right in the middle of town.

"Billy, this is spooky, this road don't go anywhere."

"I don't guess it needs to, Wayne, we are here; and this is where we were going," I said.

"That ain't what I mean...don't you feel like we have rode into a trap, with no way out?"

Maybe I didn't feel what Wayne felt. I was too busy looking for a café and hotel. I turned my horse, and started over to a crudely fashioned building with a sign hanging above the door: Pierce's Café. I pulled up at the hitching rail and started to dismount.

Wayne followed and pulled up beside me and asked, "You sure you don't feel boxed in, or strange?"

"Ah, you are just hungry, maybe you will feel some different when you get some groceries under your belt."

I held the door for Wayne, and he and I eased on inside. The place looked perfectly normal to me; the floor was laid in brick, and not too level. Enough tables and chairs filled the place, and a back door led, hopefully, to the kitchen. There were a few cowboys sitting around eating, and some just drinking beer, I suppose, in mugs. I took a table with my back to the wall, and not too far from the front door; I had read this tactic in a book. Doc Holiday said that it had saved his life more than a dozen times. Wyatt Earp advised that at least some drunk cowboy couldn't shoot you in the back.

Other than our dried out chaps and the jingling of our spurs, the place was quiet as church. The silence was soon broken by one of the cowboys sitting across the room.

"Alethea! You got some business out front!" In a flash, a lady came dashing from the back room, dressed in a long, flowery skirt and a very low cut, white blouse. She looked all around, smiled, and headed for our table, slinging a rag. Before saying a word, she leaned between us and started wiping the table.

"What can I get for you men, today?" she asked, stepping back from the table, looking us up and down.

"How about today's special, what is it?" I asked.

"The same as it was yesterday an' the day before - beef stew...an' it is very good - big chunks of beef. It's Chan's special recipe. It's all you can eat, I promise, and comes with a big chunk of corn bread I baked myself."

"We'll take it, and black coffee."

She curtsied and was off to the kitchen. I took the lady to be in her middle thirties, dark skin an' very attractive, some what hippy. It was her big ear rings that caught my attention, and so did her breasts. I just hope I wasn't staring. I don't know what had gotten into me ,here lately, guess I might be growing up, or need to start back reading my Bible.

Alethea was right; it was a plate full of cow, and a chunk of cornbread that was worth writing home about.

"Are you gonna bless our vittles, or do we just dig in?" Wayne asked, catching my gaze.

"Bless this food, O' Lord. Amen!" I uttered sharply.

Wayne chuckled under his breath, "You must be hungry, too."

"Can I get you anything else?" the young lady asked, coming back over to our table with a coffee pot.

"Some information!" I said. smiling. Alethea quickly looked toward the three cowboys sitting near our table.

"I don't know, mister, we don't get many strangers in here asking questions."

"I was just wanting to know if you know a young lady about your age named Gladys Hardy?" I guess she answered the question by the way she spun quickly around and left our table, not saying a word.

"What do you make of that?" I asked Wayne. "I think we've found the right forest."

"Yes, but we may be barking up the wrong tree" He said, looking toward the kitchen, watching the place clear completely out. I looked all around; there was not a living soul in the dining part of this place. Then, I got the strange feeling that Wayne had been talking about. By this time we were through eating; I took my last swig of coffee and got up. I started over to the counter by the back room, to pay for our meal. As I waited at the counter, I rang the little bell that was sitting there.

Suddenly a voice came from the back, "Just leave, cowboys, you don't owe us a thing."

I looked at Wayne. "Keep an eye on that front door, we're in that box you were talking about.

I stepped into the kitchen, and there found Alethea, and a Chinese man, squatting down in a corner of the kitchen.

"What's going on here?" I asked, snatching her up from the floor.

She began to shake her head and tremble all over. I turned my attention toward the Chinese cook who sat in a fetal position, shaking all over.

"He can't talk, mister, he has no tongue. They even shot a .45, holding it beside his head, bursting both ear drums. Chan can neither hear what you say to him."

"Who did this to him, was it Max Pierce?"

She slid back down in the corner and covered her head with a dish towel.

"Come on, Wayne; let's go out the back door. Go ahead and draw your Colt, and shoot the first man you see move."

This was one time I wished I was wearing two pistols. We started around the stucco building. "You look right, and I will keep an eye left, partner. As he and I came into the clearing, I could tell we surprised the three cowboys. They were expecting us to come out the front door. All three went for their guns... it was no contest. I punched out, emptied, and filled my cylinder again, not knowing what or who might hear the shots and come running.

I walked over to the three cowboys and made sure they were dead and not laying there on the ground suffering, or playing 'possum.

"I'm going back inside to get a cup of coffee and talk to Alethea."

I guess shooting and killing was normal practice in Oak Hill. We saw no one even stick their head out a door, or walk out on the street.

"I killed the three cowboys out front; did they mean anything to you or the old Chinese man?" The girl started to get up, shaking her head. The old man also eased up, and started washing dishes. "Give me and Wayne another cup of coffee, we need to have a serious talk. He and I will be out front."

We took a table where we could keep watch on the front door. Alethea brought two cups of coffee and sat down between us.

"You two don't know what you're getting yourselves into; you will never make it out of Oak Hill alive. This should be called Boot Hill."

"Why did you leave in such a hurry when we mentioned Gladys Hardy's name. You do know her, don't you?"

I thought Alethea was going to clam up on us, she looked all around. "Yes sir, she was brought to the silver mine about four months ago by Lesley Lingo, the meanest man that ever lived. Did you know that Max Pierce pays a hundred dollars for a good healthy woman to work in the big kitchen at the silver mine?"

I looked over at Wayne. He shook his head; I hoped he wasn't thinking the same thing I was.

"This is the first we've heard of a silver mine. How many men do you think this ol' man has working for him in the mine?"

"I've heard as many as twenty, 'course someone gets killed everyday, one way or the other?"

"Now we know where all the homesteaders are disappearing to. You think you and I ought to call in for extra help?"

Alethea spoke up quick, "I would think twice before I did that! There is no one you can trust around here any more, including the Texas Rangers, and especially the government. As far as I know, they are all working for Max Pierce, or taking bribes under the table."

I looked at Billy, "What do you think?"

With a disgusted look he took a swig of coffee. "I think she's right, we are in over our head, and you and I have got to dig our way out, using a six-gun instead of a shovel."

"I can tell you one thing," she said, "If, or when, you go through those big iron gates back down the road, everyone you come in contact with works for Max Pierce and are hired killers."

"What about the undertaker up the street?"

"No, he is pretty much on his own, he has never went along with the law breaking technique that Max Pierce subscribes to."

"Then you think we can trust him to keep his mouth shut, and bury these men lying out front?"

"I do."

"Me and Wayne is going up in the hills to hide out and work at night; we will stay in touch."

And with those choice words we mounted up and left town - knowing that the news would soon be out. Wayne and I knew we were between a rock and a hard place, as far as our health was concerned. The first thing he and I did was take to the woods, staying in cover as much as we could, to keep from being seen.

We found a perfect spot before dark, even the horses were hidden and had grass to nibble on, not to mention the water running down out of the rocks. You could say we were high and dry, and not that far from the silver mine, as we saw it. We were up bright and early the next morning, ready to go to work scouting out the surroundings to see what odds we were up against.

Wayne and I drew near the entrance of the silver mine, lying low. We mapped out our strategy, watching very closely when the workers came to the mine and left for the evening. There weren't that many guards to contend with.

That night as we fixed supper, mostly opened up cans that Wayne had brought, we discussed our plans.

"If you and I could close that silver mine, it would certainly put a kink in ol' Max Pierce's plans, wouldn't it?" Wayne said, laughing, "and I can tell you how we can do it plain and simple." He then went on eating, as if he had a mind relapse.

"Well, are you going to tell me, or have I got to sit here and guess?" I could tell now, Wayne had something up his sleeve besides his arm.

"Do you remember when you sent Miller Davis to get the dynamite we buried in front of the jail house?"

"Don't tell me you still have some of that dynamite?"

"Shore do!" said Wayne," two full sticks we had left over. I didn't know what to do with it, so I stuck it in my saddlebag, meaning to throw it away the next time I was out in the woods."

"Well, I'm glad you didn't, it will come in handy tonight. As soon as they load all the workers on the wagons an leave with them, you and I will ease down and close the mine."

"Won't it just make it harder on the mine workers? You know the guards will have orders to reopen it."

"At least the workers will be out in the fresh air for several days. That will give us time to get rid of the guards and gunslingers one at a tim,." I added.

"And have you gave it any thought to how we are going to do that?" Wayne asked, pulling out his bed roll.

"I haven't thought about it until just now. But don't you think, no further than the saloon is from the silver mine bunk house, that the trusted men would patronize the joints in town ,occasionally."

"You ain't talking about picking them off like ducks on a pond, are you?"

"No, Wayne! You know me better than that, we do still have several pair of handcuffs don't we?"

"Yes, we do, but getting them on the outlaws, why I'd rather pick ticks off a mountain lion's ear."

"You may get the chance to do that, too, up there where we'll be sleeping," I said laughing.

"You could've talked all day long without saying that."

"Didn't you know that a mountain lion is more scared of us than we are of them?"

"Well...if I'm ever pounced upon by a mountain lion, an' he's standing over me with slobber running from his pearly, sharp teeth - I'm gonna remind him of what you said."

We went ahead and spruced up our camp with more rocks and wood we found lying around. We were hoping it would be impossible for anyone to find us. Wayne and I planned how we would close the mine, and bide our time, until we saw all the workers leave the mine

Again, he and I would use the same procedure we had used to blow up the dynamite at the jail. As he an' I went into the mine, we found a lantern. We lit it to be able see the two sticks of dynamite once we walked out of the dark mine. We made sure we were far enough from the debris falling from the blast. Wayne injected a cartridge into the Henry magazine, and steadied his aim on a boulder a ways in front of the mine, then pulled the trigger. It did three things: it jarred the ground for miles, closed the mine, and put me and Wayne scurrying back to our hiding place.

We stayed out of sight, knowing several of the men would come back looking to see what happened. They did, then stood in front of the mine scratching their heads before mounting up an' riding off. No telling what tomorrow would hold...a good night's sleep was what I was interested in, now. I went to sleep thinking about Wayne's mountain lion.

The next morning we were real cautious with the camp fire, hoping no one would see the smoke, or smell the salt meat frying. As we suspected, the whole crew of men was at the mine working. Wayne and I got our first glimpse of Max Pierce, sitting down below in his surrey, acting as if he were cock-of-the-Walk. It took all I could do to keep Wayne from blowing his head off even with his shoulders. It was a perfect shot for his rifle. He and I had to keep reminding ourselves that we had to uphold the law, not break it. But sometimes all snakes look alike. Actually, we were too far away to hear what was going on, so we just sat tight n' quiet until Max Pierce left with three of his body guards.

"Billy, I don't know if you have noticed or not, but there is only two men down there to guard all those men."

"I see what you mean, I believe now is the time to break the men free. You got a plan?"

"Yeah, but they never work."

"Well, let's hear it anyway."

"We will ease down as close as we can, and one of us will lay down on the ground and start moaning an' groaning, like we might have got hurt in the mine explosion last night."

"And so."

"And so, the other will get behind a rock, and knock the guard in the head when he comes snooping by, to see who's hurt."

"Who is gonna lay on the ground?"

"You are, I can hit harder than you can, an' besides, it was my idea."

Wayne and I slowly made our way down the slope to find an ambush point; we found the perfect spot where I could lie and watch below. I began to moan and groan louder and louder until someone heard my cry for help. 'Course it was one of two guards. The guard that was closest started up the hill toward us; he was toting a rifle and smoking a cigarette. Wayne's plan was being executed perfectly.

"What's wrong with you, boy?" he asked as Wayne stepped from behind a bolder and cracked him over the head with an oak limb about four feet long.

"I believe you killed him," I said, getting up.

"I tried to," Wayne answered, "what are we going to do with the other one?"

I thought - this could either be a problem, or the solution.

"Well, don't you think he'll wonder what happened to the other guard, and wander off up here looking for him?" I answered.

Most of the men had stop moving rocks and were looking up our way. Curiosity got the better of the other guard, and here he came. We both hid and got ready. By now he could see his buddy lying on the ground face down.

"What happened, Fred?" he questioned.

He quickly looked around to see who had stepped out from behind the boulder. Wayne was already in his swing, and caught the man somewhere above his shoulders. He laid him, out bleeding from the mouth an' long nose; he was piled up right beside the other fellow.

Chapter Seventeen

Releasing All The Prisoners

By this time, the workers had begun to migrate up through the rocks to where we were.

"You do know other men will be here soon with dinner, don't you? I'm Roger Dykes, what can I do to help? All these men have been prisoners who've been made to work like slaves in the silver mine."

I observed more than half of the men running in all directions, as they discovered their freedom.

"You men are free to go!" I shouted. Some of the men had been kept here so long they were brainwashed, and actually didn't know what to do on their own.

"Go and hide until the wagon comes to bring lunch." There were about six men out of the twenty or so in their right minds; they were sticking with us, to help.

"We got two rifles. Take the pistols an' gun belts off the men on the ground. How many men do you think will come with the wagon?"

"Usually two, the men that serve lunch are slaves, just as we are."

Soon we saw the chow wagon approaching, with two riders on each side as escorts.

"They will park right over there in the shade. We have an hour off for lunch."

All the men with guns were waiting in the brush and rocks as the wagon pulled up and stopped. Before we had time to say a word, the sounds of a small war broke out. The two men on horseback fell to the ground, full of bullet holes. I guess they were getting revenge for all the beatings they had taken from these two men.

"Can two or three of you men with guns go up there," I pointed up the hill, "and get the two men that was guarding you a while ago? I sure wouldn't want them to wake up and run an' tell ol' Max Pierce that we are taking over his silver mine."

I waited and nobody moved. I looked at Roger Dykes.

"Well?"

He just stood there and then remarked, "I don't think those two will run off and tell anyone about nothing."

"Why?"

"They must have woke up and cut each other's throats."

"Yeah, I was afraid that might happen when I left them up there unattended to. How many of Max Pierce's men is guarding the ranch house where he lives?" I asked.

"There will be two guarding the gate coming in, and two setting on the front porch of the ranch house; I might add, all these men are excellent shots."

"We have eight guns between all us men. Do you think we can storm the house without anyone getting hurt?"

I could tell these men had hate in their hearts, and it would be difficult for me and Wayne to keep from getting hurt ourselves.

"You men take care of the front, and Wayne and I will come through the back door, and take what we came for."

I knew the men were curious to know what we came for.

Wayne spoke up, "One woman, named Gladys Hardy. Do any of you know her? She is my sister-in-law."

"I do, and if you will give her a gun she will empty it on ol' Max Pierce. He killed her newborn baby, in cold blood. He said that a person working for him had no place for a squalling brat."

"You men go ahead and eat lunch, and give us some space. We'll have to break camp, an' pack a few things and get our horses. We'll be right back."

When we came back the men were ready to go; the ones with guns were in the chuck wagon. They said they were going to make a surprise attack.

"That's good thinking. Me and Wayne will ride up to the house from behind, and come in the back door."

We found out that evening that four of Max Pierce's bodyguards had ridden into town for a few drinks, and girl pleasure. There were eight angry men with guns in the covered chuck wagon. The driver stopped right in front of the big ranch house, and I'm sorry to say, they took no prisoners. Only Max Pierce was standing at the front door, looking out. I think he suspected his goose was cooked.

"Don't go for your gun, old man, I'll kill ya right where you stand!" I announced loudly.

He hung his head and walked over and sat down in a big leather, covered chair, not saying a word. Wayne had found Gladys, his sister-in-law, in the kitchen part of the big house, and they were talking ninety to nothing.

By this time five or six of the men came rushing through the front door, into the room where I was holding a pistol on Max Pierce. And what they were saying to him is not safe to write in this book. They wanted to carry him outside and string him up. It took some talking to hold them off.

"Listen, men, I know there is no way you will be reimbursed for what you have lost. I've done heard how some of you have lost family, home, time, and only God knows the mental anguish. I understand some of you have been held hostage for nearly two years, by this sinful, murdering man, but let the law hang him legal."

By now about ten of the men that we had set free were present and accounted for. I guess the other ten or so were just proud to be free, and were still running.

Wayne and I had explained to the men that he was a deputy from Fort Worth, and I was the son of William Blunt, the U.S. Marshal.

"Now, men, listen up, all assets will be split up between you. And I understand that a big load of silver is to be shipped tomorrow. We will hold the shipment and divide it evenly, with you men that are left."

"Let me say something, as well. Gladys was just telling me that the man setting right there..." Wayne pointed to Max Pierce who was still sitting in the big chair with his head down, "she says he has two big vaults in this house that are loaded with gold and silver coins, not to mention the paper money."

I walked over to Max Pierce. Although there was a living room full of people, it was deathly quiet all of a sudden. "Get up, old man, and open that vault sitting over there by that piano."

He got up, still not saying a word. He made his way over to the rather large safe, more or less fell on his knees, and took hold of the circular dial and began to turn - first to the right, and then to the left. He stopped and turned the handle, opening the safe, and slowly got back up. The safe was chock full of money.

"Where is the other safe?" I asked.

Without saying a word, he turned and started toward two French style glass doors that led into a den. The room was full of mounts - everything from mule deer to buffalo, even a full size mountain lion, along with pheasants and many ducks.

It was rather dark in the den where the large vault stood, and not many men went in with us to open the vault. As he stood there turning the big dial, we weren't paying too much attention to the opening of the big door; I guess everyone else was as interested in the paintings and mounts hanging on the wall, as I was. Well, as soon as the big, heavy door was opened wide enough for the arm of Max Pierce, he turned around facing us, with a .45 Colt peacemaker's barrel stuck in his mouth. All I can say is, I hope he's at peace now. Two of the men standing nearby thought fast and covered his head with some dust covers off a chair, then toted him to the front porch, with the other dead men.

Gladys and another girl had put on a big pot of coffee, and we all gathered back in the big living room, where there was ample space, and plenty of chairs, to sit. On the whole, the men that had been held captive here against their wills, were mostly silent, saying very little. It was like they were in a daze, or a trance of some sort. They couldn't believe what they were seeing or hearing. Most of the men had seen much sickness and starvation in the silver mine and just figured they would be next.

"I know I'm only a sixteen year old boy...but will be a year older next week; I know I'm not the sharpest knife in the kitchen drawer, but for now, I am the spokesperson for this group of men and women alike. Let us get this through our heads, me and Deputy Wayne is the only law represented here. We are not a vigilante committee or an ungodly bunch of men, here to take over; I suggest we conduct ourselves as such."

The men seem to be in one accord, going along with what I was saying. Wayne was so pleased to find his sister-in-law alive, he wasn't saying much.

"First of all, I will need three groups of volunteers for a few jobs that are pressing...we need a group of men for a burial committee to bury the eight men that has been killed, do I see any hands?" I waited. "I guarantee you, men... each one of you will be well paid for the job."

Over half the men raised their hands. There was one big man sitting right in front of me who raised his hand. I took a step forward and laid my hand on his shoulder.

"What's your name, sir?" I asked

"John Lipton, I've been here over six months."

"Well, I'm appointing you to head up this committee; you know where everything is around here, and more 'n likely, where to bury the men." He stood up and nodded in agreement. "In that case, take the men that you will need to do the job, and get to it. When you have finished, I hope to have supper well on its way. This brings me to my next choice group of volunteers...who would like to butcher a steer for a steak supper tonight?" I could tell the men were starved for some real food. "I saw some prize beef out in the fields as I come in. What's your name, sir?" I pointed to a man standing to one side that looked like he could handle the job.

"My name is Mickey Paul, and I've been the cook for this bunch of men for over a year around here."

"I think you are our man of the hour; you head up this group and put these men to work." I walked over where Deputy Wayne was sitting beside Gladys. "It's still early, let's take the rest of the men, with their guns, an' ride into town and finish up what we've started."

Wayne started getting up, and turned to Gladice and smiled, "Deputy Billy an' I will be right back, we've got an invisible hedge all around us." He then turned and followed me and the other men out onto the front porch.

"It looks like plenty of good horses in the corral out back; I'm sure you can find saddles and blankets. I counted heads after we got underway; there were four men. Counting Deputy Wayne and myself, there were six of us. I didn't have to give these men a pep talk; they all had blood in their eyes. There wasn't a man riding with us that hadn't been beaten within an inch of his life, several times over, and the men that had gone to town to party it up, were the men we were after.

The first place we stopped was the makeshift saloon. It was a poor excuse for a building. The inside wasn't big enough to curse a cat out. The piano looked as if it came off Noah's Ark, and half the keys were stuck. The ol' bag that was trying to sing 'My Bonnie Lies Over the Ocean', sounded like she was drowning in it. She had so much make-up smeared on, one could have scraped it off with a putty knife. The whole front of her dress was missing, and I've seen better legs on a kitchen table.

"Cover me, Wayne; I'm going to get the racket stopped."

I made my way up to the piano where all the noise was coming from. I leaned over and asked the man who was sitting on the stool, wearing a derby hat and smoking a cigar, to knock it off; I had an announcement to make. He never even looked my way, but got louder.

I yelled as loudly as I could, into his ear, "I said stop playing, I have an announcement to make."

I felt someone catch hold of my shirt and snatch; it was the woman singer. She caught my gaze and smiled, every other tooth was missing. I quickly thought, I'll bet she has a time trying to eat English peas.

"Oliver, can't hear nothing, sonny boy, he can't even hear his self break wind, the only way he knows...is when he smells the stench." I thought, surely this can't go on much longer. "You want us to stop while you make your announcement?"

"Yes, ma'am, it won't take me long, then you can finish... I just love that song and the way you sing it."

She quickly reached down and grabbed the piano player's hand. He looked up and she shook her head, and he quit playing.

I backed up against the hardwood bar, to keep from getting shot in the back.

"Is anyone settin' in here that works for ol' man Max Pierce?"

I had no idea that Lesley Lingo, the man that killed Wayne's brother-in-law and brought Gladys to Oak Hill, was sitting in the crowd of six or eight men, on the other side of the saloon. No sooner than the words left my mouth, four men stood up. I took it that one of the men was Lesley Lingo.

"And just what business is it of yours, kid? I see you are imitating a gunslinger, with that Colt hanging low on your side."

And those were the last words he uttered this side of hell. When his shoulder moved, I drew and fanned two shots in his direction and down he went, taking the table with him. The other men with us had made their way inside and were mad as hell. I guess they recognized most of Max Pierce's men. Sad to say, it was a blood bath. Two of our men took a bullet, but nothing serious. Nine of Max Pierce's men lay dead on the floor. The lead singer, with all the make-up, came over after the shooting was over and apologized; she said she just wasn't up to singing the song 'I loved so much.

News travels fast in a one horse town with one road in and no way out. I guess Alethea was right, maybe the name needed to be changed to Boot Hill, instead of Oak Hill. We rode out just like we rode in. A handful of men, good men, had set a town free. It was for sure the undertaker of Oak Hill was going to have his hands full tonight and all-day tomorrow!

"Wayne, you and the others go ahead to the ranch, I'm going to swing by the café and give Alethea and Chan the good news."

I made my over to the café, dismounted and walked in with high spirits. Both the kitchen and café part was as empty as a purple martin box in December. What has happened, I wondered, did Max Pierce suspect Alethea or old Chan of snitching on him and his illegal shenanigans in Oak Hill and the silver mine? Well, he was dead now... and buried I hoped; there was nothing more I could do...I could give Alethea and Chan the café to keep open, if they wanted it.

I began to look all around. There was no blood or turned over tables, and no broken dishes in the kitchen. I moved slowly out of the café with mixed emotions. Just I started to throw a leg over the saddle, I caught a glimpse of something in the brush behind the café. At first I thought it might have been trash; there was certainly enough scattered out back. At second glance, I saw movement back deeper in the bushes. I quickly straddled my saddle an' kicked my mount in the ribs, turning his head toward the moving object in the brush, only to find Alethea and Chan crawling on their hands and knees - like a bob white quail trying to slip out on a lemon pointer.

"Where do you think you are going?" Alethea stopped and looked back. I could tell she was scared - almost hysterical.

"Me and Chan heard all the shooting over at the saloon and thought Max Pierce was letting his men kill everyone in town.

"Max Pierce and all of his men are dead. Come on and go with me over to the livery stable; I will get you a buck board. I want you and Chan to go down to Max Pierce's ranch house with me. Supper should be well on the way. After supper, we are going to divide up all his fortune, and probably give you and Chan the café, that is if you want it."

We could hear the laughter and smell the beef steaks cooking before we reached the ranch house. Soon after supper and everyone had eaten his or her fill, and were still "soaking in" the fact that they were free to go or to stay. One of the men, by the name of Homer Travick, said he wished he could stay on and run the silver mine; it was the only life he knew. Still others wanted to stay on and manage the ranch, and raise beeves.

I could detect this day had changed the lives of many men. They had seen the light; there was a future ahead of them. In the next two days, before Deputy Wayne and I myself set saddle on our way back to Fort Worth, he and I saw a new town form out of the men and women of Oak Hill; there were no big I and little you There was a new mayor, sheriff, and seven city council members elected. It appeared that everyone was in one accord as we said goodbye that morning. Deputy Wayne and Gladys seemed to have inherited a fine surrey that had belonged to "you know who". And it was noised that Gladys would no longer be Deputy Wayne's sister-in-law, but his wife, that is, as soon as they could find a preacher.

Gladys had received her share of the fortune from the estate of Max Pierce. As the new city council members were going through Max Pierce's important papers, they found he had money in three different banks - some in Houston, Dallas, and also Fort Worth. A lawyer was called in to head up the new government of Oak Hill to make everything legal and above board.

On the last night before leaving Oak Hill, I turned seventeen. As I ate my cake, I couldn't believe this was all actually happening. The crowd began to cheer as I was presented a birthday present. As I tore the paper off the mahogany box, I found that it contained two pearl handled, nickel plated, engraved, Colt .45 peacemaker pistols. They worth a small fortune. The next present I unwrapped was a gun belt. What could I say? I had only seen this one in a magazine I had read some time ago. The shiny gold and silver, and even some rare stones glittered as I tried it on; it was a perfect fit. Of course, the gun rigging was all part of Max Pierce's gun collection.

Wayne said jokingly, as the three of us rode into Fort Worth and parted company, "It's good to be back in one piece, safe and sound." He and Gladys went their way.

I was long overdue a good bath and seeing my folks. I turned my horse northward and went home. My, my - how glad they were to see me! It took me the rest of the day and evening to tell my parents what I had been through, and what had happened in Oak Hill, Texas after I had arrived there. Mother said it was hard to believe men were still used for slave labor. I could tell Father wasn't surprised one bit.

"Well, Son, you haven't even asked how your father is faring, since you've been here."

"Oh, Mother, I'm sorry! I just took for granted you were okay, Father, up walking around."

Mother's countenance changed, and the smile left her face. "Your father is not okay."

I was caught by surprise, and looked at Father. The smile left his face as he turned in his chair, "Doctor Childers has given me some bad news... you tell him, Elizabeth." Father turned his head.

"Your Father has no use of his right arm' and it is getting worse everyday."

"This can't be, Mother, Doctor Childers is wrong with his diagnosis!" Both Mother and Father started shaking their heads at the same time. "What are we going to do?" I asked, almost starting to shed a few tears in sorrow.

"Your father has already done what he had to do." Mother looked at Father, and took him by the hand.

"That's right, Son, I sent a telegram to Governor Davis and resigned my position as U.S. Marshal, yesterday."

"But, Father, that can't be!"

"I afraid it is, Billy, me and your mother are selling out and moving back east."

"But, Father an' Mother, you haven't heard my plans yet!."

"You know, Billy...we don't allow 'buts' in this family."

"I know, Mother, how well I know; will you both allow me one just one little 'but'?" They said nothing, then nodded their approval.

"I'm going with you. I'm enrolling in college this fall an' will go as long as it takes to become a good Doctor. I wanted to tell you both, before Wayne an I left for Oak Hill last week."

"I guess you know, Billy, this wasn't in the governor's plans."

"I know, I don't work for the governor," I said, looking over at Mother. She started crying. I laid my hand on her arm. "We kinda all got what we wanted, except Father."

"Don't worry about me, I'm over the hill anyway," Father said, making a trip to the coffee pot.

"William, I could have gotten that for you," Mother said, wiping her eyes.

"You see, Billy, Elizabeth is already waiting on me hand and foot. Let me go see who is at the front door, at least I'm able to do that."

As far as looking at Father, you couldn't tell there was anything wrong with him. Mother and I were still talking when Father came back into the kitchen with a frightful look on his face, holding his cup of coffee, and shaking all over.

"Good Lord, Father, what's wrong with you?" I asked.

"Let me sit down!" he answered, hyperventilating some what.

"Did you see a ghost at the door?" Mother asked, starting to get up.

"No, no, stay here, my Elizabeth!"

"I'll see who it is, an' be right back!" I jumped up and started to the front door. As I passed Father he grabbed my shirt with his left hand, and nearly pulled my shirt tail out of my britches.

"No, Billy, he has come to kill you!"

"Kill me?"

"That's what he said, I didn't get all he was saying, but it had something to with Oak Hill last week."

"You can't go out there, Son, let me go out there and talk to him!" Mother exclaimed.

"I remember now... he said he was Lesley Lingo's boy and was on a cattle drive out of town when you killed his pa."

"I do remember someone in Oak Hill mentioning his name in passing. They said they hoped I never had to face him. His father, a famous gunfighter, had trained his son well."

"No, Billy!" Mother pleaded. "There must be some other way."

"There is no other way, Mother; I made my bed and now I've got to sleep in it."

I pulled out my Colt and made sure all six cylinders were loaded, then dropped it back in my holster.

"Mother, you pray that hedge a little higher around me. I'm going out the back door and surprise him." I felt a hand on my back as I eased out the back door.

I swung wide as I came around our house, I was gathering some distance between him and me. He might be faster, but I was more accurate at a distance. I was at least fifty yards from him when I stopped to make my play. He had never noticed me; it was late and I had on dark clothes. I could tell he had his eyes glued to the front door, ready to draw and shoot. I knew his tactics; I had read about gunslingers like him...to get the first shot off was his plan.

"You looking for me?" I called out. He wheeled and drew, firing the first shot... I drew and fired. I heard Mother scream; she was standing at the front door with Father and saw the white puff of smoke come from my opponent's pistol first. We both were still standing and looking at each other. In a split second, his Colt fell to the ground in our front yard. His knees buckled under him and he fell to the grass and never moved again.

As I neared the front porch where Mother and Father stood, I punched the empty casing out of my six gun and handed it to Mother; it was still warm.

"Keep this as a souvenir, and pray this is the last man I have to kill."

Mother gathered both me and father in her loving arms, and hugged us all together.

I saw something that day I had never seen; I knew my father was a big man, but I saw a big, big man that evening. My father broke down and cried like a whipped baby. Mother and I managed to get Father back into the living room and seated on the couch.

"You think I need to go fetch Doc Childers?" I asked Mother.

"No," she said, "he has already told me your father would have days like this."

"Is this why you and he want to go back east?" I asked.

"This is part of it, Son, your father and I are going where no one knows us. There is not a day that passes that your father's life is not threatened in some way or the other. Many men he has sent to prison claim they will kill him when they get out of prison. He and I can't take this any longer; it has affected your father's mental state in many ways."

It seemed to soothe both Father's and Mother's spirits just telling me this.

"Billy, we know that we can triple our money on the house, the way Fort Worth has grown. And the hardware store - we can ask our own price. We'll not be hurting financially in any way."

"Then I take it you and Father plan to move soon?"

"The sooner the better."

Chapter Eighteen

Going Back East

You could say Mother was right. The hardware store was no trouble to sell; and Lewis Bradley, the new man that Father had hired to fix guns and work in the hardware store, wanted to buy the gun shop and all the tools. He also wanted to move it into his own building. Father said that was fine with him.

Now the house was a little harder to sell. Mother ran ads in the Eastern newspapers, hoping that some fool with lots of money wanted to move west. I could tell Mother wasn't overjoyed by our move to Fort Worth, two years ago. But new hope had arrived when she found out I was going to quit this 'foolishness', as she called it, and go to an eastern college.

Father never said anything, but something inside of me...maybe a gut feeling, if you will, said he felt it was the biggest mistake of his entire life - moving out west, only to get crippled up, and spend the rest of his life being waited on. No-sir-ree, this wasn't Father's cup of tea at all. But there was no one he could blame but himself, and this he would probably carry to his grave.

It had been a month since I came back from Oak Hill, and I thought the matter was finished, the case was closed, and everyone was doing well. And from all indications, it was. But the big news over the telegraph this morning was a prison break last night. And according to the warden, all of the bunch of men with Walter King had broken out of prison, and were headed back to Fort Worth to settle some unfinished business. Now, one didn't have to be a Philadelphia lawyer to see the writing on the wall. If you ask me, they were going to ride in here and settle the score with the U.S. Marshal, and anybody else that had anything to do with them going to prison.

This could very well be the straw that broke the camel's back, if Father got wind of this. I talked to Mother in private, and she thought it might put Father over the edge. All I can say is that me and Deputy Wayne had our work cut out for us; 'course there was Miller Davis, who was still no help.

Now the way I figured it, that bunch of polecats would have to come to town before they could do any damage. The only thing we didn't know was when they would come. But we had time to formulate a plan. I walked back into the jail, where Miller had put on a fresh pot of coffee and Deputy Wayne was waiting to drink it all up.

"You got any ideas what we are up against with Walter King's bunch of skunks?"

Deputy Wayne was sitting at the desk; he spun around as if he had an idea.

"You want me to get some more dynamite?" Miller asked, bringing the coffee pot in the main office of the jail.

"Now, let me ask you two, if you were going to try to kill the marshal, how would you go about doing it? Think hard," I reached for my cup.

"Well, it's for sure I wouldn't come barging into town and start shooting!" Miller exclaimed.

"You're right, Miller, I believe they will slip in unnoticed and get the job done, then head for Mexico," said Wayne

"So, we are right back where we started, except they got to get close enough to the marshal to shoot him," I observed.

"First of all, they probably don't think we know about them breaking out of prison yet," Wayne added

"I'm sure they had outside help, and it's for sure they got horses by now, an' are well on their way here," I responded.

"Wouldn't you think they'd have a posse on their tail right now, and this alone will put them a little off guard?" questioned Wayne.

"You are saying they may do something stupid, like not being too careful in their thinking."

"Don't you think they know the marshal is practically bedridden?"

"I don't know about that, they just want him dead," I said.

"You know what I believe?" We both looked at Miller. "I believe they will hit at night, over at the house."

"You're right about one thing, Miller, if they plan on shooting Father, it will be over at the house."

"But Miller may have a point; I bet you they will strike tomorrow night, especially if they are crowded by the posse."

"Billy, I think that would be easy enough to take care of," remarked Wayne. He poured himself another cup of coffee.

"Well?" I said, waiting.

"Well! We'll hide over in your front yard until they make their play. According to the almanac, the moon will give us favor," Wayne answered, as he walked over and sat down behind the homemade desk. He propped up one foot.

"We'll take those two double barreled shotguns hanging up there; they will give us more favor."

"Especially if you load them with some double O buckshot," Miller said, laughing.

"You mean just shoot 'em down like a mangy coyote?" questioned Wayne.

"No! More like the rabid dogs that they are; they are here to kill the marshal, ain't they?"

Wayne and I spent the rest of the day planning out our strategy and going over the pros and cons of this covert operation. We were not letting the marshal in on our plans. Miller and I cut some brush from the back and added it to a flower bed in the yard, so we could be completely hidden from our intruders. 'Course it looked more like a duck-blind when we finished. But what would they know? It would be dark.

With nothing more to do with our time Deputy Wayne and I selected a weapon off the wall - a twelve gauge double barreled shotgun. We oiled it up and made sure it would shoot, and started the waiting game.

"Do you really think they will try to kill the marshal?" Wayne asked.

"I really do believe so; I saw the hate in those men when we put then in jail," I replied.

"When do you want to go over to your house to get in the blind and wait?"

I could tell Wayne was ready to apprehend this slime once again.

"Sometime soon after dark; we don't want to be seen, or blow our cover, that's for sure. I tell you what, let's go to Joe's Café an' eat us a good supper just before they close, an' we should be ready."

Wayne thought that was a good idea.

"Can I go and eat with you guys," asked Miller.

"We don't mind, the more the merrier, I think the city fathers should pay for it anyway," I suggested, with both Wayne an' Miller saying 'amen'.

As we three sat eating supper, dinner as Mother calls it, I could tell Wayne and Miller, and I guess me included, had some doubt they would show.

"You don't think we're wasting our time, do you?" I asked.

Wayne looked at Miller. "I don't think we've wasted our time, even if they don't show up. How would we ever know? And what if they did break in on your folks, Billy, and harm your pa? I could never forgive myself," Wayne said, pushing his plate back and rubbing his belly.

"Well, thanks, Brother Billy, that sure hit the spot," Miller commented, as he starting to get up from the table.

"Don't thank me, thank the town council. They are the ones that have got to cough up the money."

"You about ready to go get in our nest? It's dark as pitch out here, but look at that full moon coming up. I guess you might as well go on back over to the jail and keep an eye on things until you hear from us," I said to Miller as we split up.

"Did you bring of plenty shells for your shotgun, Billy?" Wayne asked, as we walked along, breathing the cool night air.

"I guess so; we're not going into a war you know. I doubt it'll be more than two or three that gets involved."

"Well, if you run out, just holler, I got both pockets full."

"Like I said, we're not going to a dove shoot, but I'm sure glad you brought that gallon jug of water."

He and I made the blind home for as long as it would take. Wayne had found two empty five gallon lard cans for us to sit on, and it made it very nice. We finished camouflaging ourselves where we could see the whole lawn and house.

A breeze had picked up and that was good; it was blowing the mosquitoes off of us; and he and I could stay still without fighting insects. I guess he and I had gotten settled in, and a hour or so had passed, when we saw two silhouettes coming our way. I heard Wayne cock his shotgun.

"Don't shoot yet!" I whispered urgently.

Whoever it was, one of them was taller than the other. And they would stop every now and then. As they came closer, we could tell it was a boy and girl, no harm, just out for an evening stroll in the cool night air. By the time they had come within a few yards of us, conversation between the two had stopped; making love was their game.

Wayne and I watched for a minute or so, hoping they would go on someplace else. But before our very eyes, and in spitting distance, they started to to spread a quilt on the grass. We knew right then and there we had a real crisis on our hands.

"Can you talk like a girl?" I whispered in Wayne's ear.

"Don't know, I have never tried." He whispered back.

"Well, just say the same thing I do."

"Okay, I'll try."

"This spot is taken, children," I said loudly, in a deep bass voice.

"Yes, this spot is taken, children!" Wayne said, in a little girl's voice. I nearly busted out laughing and almost fell off the lard can. I thought to myself, what would an old man and a young girl be doing over in a flower bed at eleven o'clock at night?

"We're sorry, sir! We're leaving right now," a voice replied.

We watched as they quickly jerked the covering from the ground and fled into the night.

"Did you know who they were?" I asked.

"I'm afraid not, Billy, there are so many new folks moving into town here lately."

"Well, Wayne, I guess this is as good a time to tell you, as any; hopefully by next week there will be three less folks in Fort Worth, Texas."

I couldn't see Wayne's face, but I detected a question in his voice. "What are you referring too?" he asked.

"We are moving back east as soon as this dilemma is over." I could tell he was caught off guard and, in the dark, literally.

"But your dad is the U.S. Marshal here in this area isn't he?"

"Not any more," I said. "He called the governor and resigned a day or two ago."

"But!"

"There is no but about it. As quick as the house is sold we're taking a train back east. I'm enrolling in a good college, and Father is buying him a new fishing pole."

"What about me?" Wayne pleaded.

"I', sure you and Gladys have future plans, and if you want some free advice, after tonight...if me and you are not killed, I would take that Colt off your side, pack it up and never look back."

"You sound plum serious, Billy!"

"I am, Wayne...look back at the past year...look how many deputies that has been killed right here in Fort Worth."

He didn't say anything for the longest. We could hear the music coming from all the saloons in town; the night life was going full blast, and I'm sure the beer and wine was flowing, also.

It was a few minutes after twelve o'clock by my watch I had cautiously struck a match to see. "Wayne, old buddy, this lard can doesn't exactly fit my rump."

"Mine either, but it's better than setting on the ground."

"I guess you're right...take a look! What is this coming our way?" Were these the men we had been patiently waiting on, or three riders coming or leaving the saloon? I thought, 'we'll soon find out', as they came closer. All of a sudden they stopped. I couldn't hear what they were saying. We waited. They began to dismount, leaving one cowboy to hold their horses. The two started across our front lawn heading toward our house. By now they were pretty much on the other side of us. The two split up and started looking in the front windows. Of course Mother had all the shades pulled completely down. The two met back right in front of our house and stood there discussing their plans.

Of course, when they stepped up on our porch, our plans went into effect.

"I wouldn't try that if I were you men!" I shouted as loudly as I could.

Might have known - they jumped off the porch and here they came, running across the lawn.

"Halt!" I screamed, "Stop, or I'll shoot!" Well, sad to say, they didn't stop, and Wayne and I unloaded two double barrel shotguns. The men fell where they were shot, and never moved. I quickly turned my attention to the man in the rear, holding the horses.

"Don't shoot!" he cried out, throwing both hands high into the air.

I walked over to where the lone stranger was standing. "Look, mister, I didn't know what these men were going to do until a few minutes ago."

"You are saying you don't know these men lying over there on the ground?"

He put his hands down, scared out of his wits. "I just met them last night. They said they was going down Mexico way, and I asked if I could ride along with them."

"Is that your horse?" I asked.

"Yes sir."

"Well, tie the other two horses to that branch hanging over there and get on your horse and get out of town before I shoot you."

That he did, and was on his way. I moseyed over where to Wayne was squatting down by the two men lying on the ground.

"What do you think?" I asked.

"Both dead now."

"You stay here and I'll go wake up Craig Watson, our undertaker."

The next morning at breakfast Mother had a wonderful meal prepared for us.

While sitting at the table, Father brought up the subject, "Was I dreaming, or did I hear gunshots about midnight?"

I looked over at Mother who twisted her mouth and replied, "You must have been dreaming, William."

The End

Other Great Books By Charlie Barnett

Amazing Grace

Cat Man Road

Dead But Not Buried

Devils, Daemons And Deliverance

Georgia Cowboy

Going Back To Abilene

Go West Young Man

Heading West

Humorous Poems & Funny Stories

I Fell In Love With My Rapist

Just Jokes

My Mother Was An Angel

Run Johnny Run

Short Stories Told By My Granny

Standing In The Shadow

Suitcase Full Of Money

Through The Bible In Poems

Youngest Gun Slinger

Website: www.gateswoodbooks.com

About The Author

Born in 1936, Charlie Barnett has lived his whole life within three acres of where he first saw the light of day. At the age of thirteen Charlie began publishing a monthly school comic book. Today, 62 years later, he has authored sixteen books with many more on the way. Charlie has also penned over 200 poems that range from inspirational to southern humor.

Before retiring, Charlie spent decades as a successful entrepreneur and minister. He enjoys writing, watching westerns, gardening, and observing butterflies and hummingbirds.

Charlie has been married to his wife, Janice, since 1958. Today they enjoy their growing family that includes four sons, eleven grandchildren and eight great-grandchildren. Charlie is always up for a good laugh, telling stories, and speaking engagements.

Visit Charlie on the web at www.gateswoodbooks.com